Buried

Treasures

Mary Manners

Mary Manners

Contact Information: titleadmin@pelicanbookgroup.com

All scripture quotations, unless otherwise indicated, are taken from the Holy Bible, New International Version(R), NIV(R), Copyright 1973, 1978, 1984 by Biblica, Inc.™ Used by permission of Zondervan. All rights reserved worldwide. www.zondervan.com

Cover Art by *Kim Mendoza*

White Rose Publishing, a division of Pelican Ventures, LLC
www.whiterosepublishing.com PO Box 1738 *Aztec, NM * 87410

White Rose Publishing Circle and Rosebud logo is a trademark of Pelican Ventures, LLC

Publishing History
First White Rose Edition, 2011
Print Edition ISBN 978-1-61116-095-6
Electronic Edition ISBN 978-1-61116-096-3
Published in the United States of America

Dedication

To Dee Dee...my sister, my friend. You are a treasure. I hope you always dance...

Also Available by Mary Manners

Mended Heart
Tender Mercies
Brenna's Choice
Light the Fire
Love's Kindled Flame

Sweet Treats Bakery Series
(Coming Soon)

Kate's Kisses
Grace's Gold
Mattie's Meltaways
Tessa's Teacakes

Praise for Mary Manners

"Mary Manners' writing is reminiscent of Karen Kingsbury"

~A. Hinshaw

"This author will be one I search out in the future"

~The Romance Studio

"This novel by Mary Manners is a real treat…a heartwarming tale you won't want to miss"

~Happily Ever After Reviews

"At the road's end, Mary Manners will leave you anticipating the next journey"

~Schwitze (Amazon.com)

"Mary Manners has a gift for weaving a love story that leaves readers wishing they could ride off into the sunset with her characters"

~Toni (Amazon.com)

Though I have fallen, I will rise. Though I sit in darkness, the Lord will be my light.

~Micah 7:8

1

Matt plopped quick-drying spackle over a crack in the wall and smoothed it with the trowel. The steady cadence of *plop, swish, scrape* blended with the easy rhythm of country music that drifted across the room and eased his frustration.

He watched Paul lift a bucket of spackle and dip his trowel, and he wondered how the kid—his nephew—had ended up on his doorstep three months ago.

Because Eydie's back in rehab again. Will it ever end?

He glanced through an expanse of dirt-splattered bay windows that opened over the battered front porch, affording an impressive view of sleepy-dawn breaking over the tawny pasture beyond. Horses grazed in the cross-fenced field, their heads bowed in search of late-winter grass to supplement sweet feed. At the far end of the field, his house sat nestled among a grove of shade trees, and beyond that a low-hanging thunderhead rolled across the sky like an angry, steel-gray tide.

"Storm's headed this way." Paul dragged a hand

1

through unruly black hair and tossed a glance at Matt. His eyes, dark and tired, said he'd slept no better last night than Matt had. "I should call Andie and tell her to put the horses in the barn."

"And wake her whole house?" Matt shook his head. "I don't think so. Come over here and finish spackling while I fix the lock on the front door. I'd like to get this done before the rain hits."

"Don't think that's gonna happen." Paul took the trowel. "Hear the wind picking up?"

"I do, but it'll be a while before the hard stuff blows through." He could smell the sweet, dank scent of rain, though. The wind swayed, moving restlessly around the house like a thief trying to find a way in. Upstairs, a broken shutter drummed against weathered clapboard siding.

"Whatever." Paul dipped the trowel into the bucket of spackle and plopped the mess onto a fissure in the wall. "I don't understand why we're fixing up this house, anyway."

"Because I promised Nora...and when I make a promise I keep it."

Paul frowned. "But she's dead, so how would she even know whether or not you kept your promise?"

*Dead...*the single word carried such power. Matt's stomach soured, and his voice turned gruff in the early-morning chill. The heat was cranked, but the ancient pump did little to slake the cold edge. He could kindle a fire in the broad stacked-stone fireplace that filled one wall of the living room, but he didn't plan on hanging around long enough for it to matter. Church service was due to start in a few hours, and he planned to be there...Paul, too.

Matt grabbed the hammer from his tool box and

turned to face Paul. The kid's flippant attitude had a way of getting under his skin. He sucked a deep breath…in…out, and gave himself a little pep talk.

Calm voice…keep your cool. Remember, he's watching you, learning from you.

When he spoke, his voice was steady. "If I didn't keep my promise *I* would know."

Paul shrugged. "Like I said, whatever." He smoothed spackle over the crack and grimaced at the radio. "Can we listen to something else? This so-called music is putting me to sleep."

"I'm waiting for the weather report."

"*I* can give you the weather report—it's gonna rain—hard. There, can I change the station now?"

"No. Spackle faster. Caroline and her daughter are due to arrive in less than a week. I want to have the cracks in the walls repaired and the rooms painted and ready for them to move in."

"Caroline?"

"Nora's niece. She's coming from Chicago."

☙❧

Caroline's spine screamed in agony as the Honda bumped over another rut in the two-lane country road. Angry clouds rumbled overhead, and the sky darkened to an oily blackness. The scent of rain filled the air and settled on her tongue. She gnawed her lower lip and squinted through eerie yellow-green darkness in search of the side road to Aunt Nora's.

It's been too long…and I've forgotten my way around here. Oh, why did Aunt Nora think leaving her old farmhouse to me was a good idea? And Aunt Nora…I can't believe you've been gone nearly six months now…I miss you

3

so!

Thunder shook the car and Caroline cringed, her knuckles white on the steering wheel. A glance into the rearview mirror told her Callie was sleeping soundly through the chaos. Her head of soft blonde ringlets slumped at an awkward angle, and the pink windbreaker tucked around her shoulders was rumpled and stained with grape juice.

Caroline swallowed hard and turned her attention back to the dark road ahead. Her voice was a murmur over the low hum of the radio. "Dear Lord, I need your help here. This car's running on fumes, and Callie's going to wake any moment. She's going to be hungry and cranky and as sick of being held prisoner in this car as I am. So, have mercy, Lord. Throw me a bone."

Wind swirled restlessly around the car as if to mock her, and the sky grew more ominous with each passing moment. Driving straight through the night while Callie slept had seemed like a good idea when she sped from Chicago...away from the memories that haunted her like a nightmare that wouldn't let go. But now, twelve hours and five hundred long miles later, she wasn't so sure.

Not that she could have stayed in Chicago another day...not with the court date looming. *What if he...that heartless killer...was released?*

The car crested a hill, and a flicker of light on the horizon caught Caroline's attention. Someone was awake in a house across the pasture. She wiped condensation from the bug-splattered windshield with the sleeve of her flannel shirt and squinted into darkness.

The car's headlights caught a sign at the next intersection. Caroline gasped. Collier Road...the road to Aunt Nora's house!

My house now...and Callie's. Her heart stuttered as she struggled to train her gaze on the house and navigate the road at the same time. What were lights doing on? Who was there...and why?

Caroline's belly knotted. Her hands trembled on the steering wheel. She prayed the gas tank held enough fuel to power the car as she eased down the winding road. Rising winds heaved the vehicle from side to side like a rag doll. A jagged bolt of lightning ripped the sky, followed by a roar of thunder that tossed her back in the seat. Bullets of rain pelted the windshield like machine-gun fire.

Please, Lord, guide Callie and me to the light.

The glow from the house grew brighter, illuminating the sleepy horizon. She followed the curve of the road and found the narrow entrance to a winding gravel drive flanked by dancing Bradford pear trees. Floodlights cast an eerie glow over the front yard, and rain blew sideways like a gush from a fire hose, blinding her. The familiar whitewashed farmhouse rose through the shadows like a winking sentinel with a peeling sunburn. A broken shutter slapped against a second-story window.

A pickup sat in the drive. Caroline slammed on the brakes. The car fishtailed, spitting gravel, and missed the pickup by mere inches before it sputtered a dying breath. Caroline heaved a sigh of relief, threw off her seatbelt, and swung around to check Callie.

"How on earth did you manage to sleep through that, baby?" Her breath came in gasps as she brushed hair from Callie's clammy forehead. "The storm's bearing down on us."

Lightning struck a Bradford near the road. Its

trunk erupted in a deafening crack followed by a shower of sparks. The acrid smell of scorched wood filled the air. Caroline shoved open the driver's door and shivered as cold rain pelted and stung, and the wind whipped her long hair into damp knots. Heart racing, she threw open the back door and wrestled Callie from her booster seat. Shielding the child's sleep-limp body, she slammed the car door and dashed through the downpour to the protection of the porch awning.

That's when she saw him through the smudged front bay windows...the man inside the house—her house. Coffee-colored hair covered the collar of his rumpled navy T-shirt, and muscles grew taught as he swung a hammer at the door frame. Staccato pounding echoed over the howl of wind that swirled around her. He was big, tall...powerful-looking. She imagined he could do a lot of damage with that hammer.

Lightning flashed around her like strobes doing battle with the floodlights over the front porch. Thunder roared and rocked the ground, nearly knocking her off her feet. In her arms, Callie whimpered and squirmed through a restless dream. Caroline fumbled in her pocket for her cell phone and realized she'd left it on the front seat of the car along with her purse...and the car keys.

Caroline debated only a moment before grabbing an industrial-sized push-broom propped against a wicker rocker near the front door. The storm closed in.

She cradled Callie in one arm and hoisted the broom handle like a saber in the other as she kicked open the solid-wood front door. The element of surprise was all she had going for her.

The door slammed wide, and the man tumbled

backwards from the force of her kick. The hammer flew from his hand. It bounced off the hearth and clattered across the scuffed wood floor behind him.

"What are you doing here?" Adrenaline had Caroline's heart galloping. Suddenly her senses came to full attention, and the exhaustion from a twelve-hour drive through night-blackness fled.

"What the…" He scrambled to his feet. Wide blue eyes gaped at her from beneath plaster-speckled hair. His face was streaked with grease, and his paint-splattered T-shirt sported a gaping rip at the hem.

"Get away. Move back toward the wall." She jabbed the broom handle at his mid-section.

He sidestepped and held up both hands. "Careful with that, Caroline."

The sound of her name eased her fear down a notch. How did he know who she was?

"I said move back." Caroline managed to hold her voice steady as she jabbed the broom at him again. A rush of adrenaline burned through her. "I mean it."

"You've got this all wrong." Shock flashed to realization. He shook his head as laughter rose from the pit of his belly, startling her. His broad shoulders shook with each breath. "You're going to scare the kid, Caroline. Give me that." He yanked the broom from her with one quick motion and tossed it to the floor behind him. "Good grief. Do you realize the danger in what you just did, barging in on me like that? If you really thought I'd hurt you, you should have gone for help, first."

Her chin rose in defiance as she cradled Callie against her. "Maybe I have. Maybe when I spotted your truck in the drive I called the police, and they're on their way right now." She should have called them, had been foolish not to. The idea caused a wave of terror to crest, but she tamped it down and bowed up to her full height, which brought her only to his shoulder. "I don't understand what's going on here. I think you should leave. Now."

"It's storming out there, in case you haven't noticed." Rain crashed against the bay windows in torrents, and the wind wailed and moaned through the open front door. He motioned to a radio on the coffee table. "Tornado watches have been issued clear across the county, Caroline, and into Knoxville."

"I'm fully aware of that." Callie whimpered and squirmed in her arms, and Caroline ached under the weight of her.

The child's eyes fluttered open. "Mama, is there gonna be a tornado?"

"No, baby." She smoothed damp hair and kissed a clammy forehead.

"But Mama—"

"Everything's fine. Go back to sleep now." Caroline shot the guy a look. "Nice going." She stuffed a trembling hand into the pocket of her jeans, as if reaching for her phone. "I'm going to speed-dial the police right now."

"Fine. You do that." His voice challenged as his gaze narrowed. "The number's nine-one-one." He crossed his arms and leaned against the wall. "But why don't you lay the kid on the couch first before you drop her?"

"Because..." Caroline recognized the flowered loveseat near the fireplace as the one she'd spent lazy teenage summer afternoons sprawled across, poring through Aunt Nora's expansive collection of novels. She sighed and drew her hand, empty, from her pocket. Her voice rose with a simple plea. "Look, I don't know what you're doing here, especially at this hour of the night, but you'd better leave. I know the neighbors across the way, and I'll get them."

"It's practically morning now." He laughed again. "And you're a week early, Caroline. Did you drive all night? What are you doing out in this weather?" Taller than her by more than a foot, he took a step toward her, and she stumbled back, drawing Callie tight to her chest. His deep blue eyes inched over her as she shivered. The width of his shoulders filled the doorframe. "Are you trying to get yourself killed?"

The words struck with more force than the clap of thunder that rocked the house. Lightning danced through the open front door, and rain splattered the hardwood floor. Caroline watched him reach for a denim jacket that had been tossed across the fireplace hearth. He smoothed the fabric and draped it over Callie. "The kid's shivering."

"How do you know my name...or that I've arrived early?" The jacket smelled like hay and damp earth mingled with a hint of clean aftershave. Caroline tucked the edges around Callie's shoulders. "Who are you, and how did you get in here?" She glanced at the splintered door frame, frowned at the gaping hole in the oak door where a handle and deadbolt should have been. "The lock's broke. Did you do that?"

"Relax. Take a breath before you hyperventilate." He kicked the door closed and took the broom from the floor to prop it against the wall. Then he sauntered across the room to pick up his hammer before turning back to face her. "I'm Matt Carlson. *I'm* your neighbor from across the pasture, and Nora asked me to take care of a few things around here."

"She did? But she's been gone…"

"I know how long she's been gone." He took a tentative step toward her. "Would you let me help you with the kid—"

Caroline scooted back. "Her name's Callie."

"Right." He took another step forward, his voice low and smooth. "Would you please let me take her? You look like you're about to collapse."

Caroline held her ground, but loosened her grip on Callie and nodded slightly. "Just to the couch, OK? And put the hammer down, first."

Matt nodded slightly, tossed the hammer into the tool box, and gathered Callie into his arms. She nestled her head against his cotton T-shirt. "There you go. That's better, sweetie." He laid her on the couch and tucked the jacket around her shoulders.

"Did you say your name is Carlson?" Caroline kept her eyes on him. His touch seemed safe and gentle as he slid a throw pillow beneath Callie's head, yet she couldn't be too sure. "But the people across the pasture were…"

"Older. I know." After readjusting the jacket over Callie, he stood to face her. "My grandparents used to live across the pasture. They retired to Knoxville a few years ago, and now I live in the house. I was a friend of Nora's. I knew you were coming, but I thought it wasn't until sometime next week."

"Change of plans." Caroline eyed the tool box. "So what's with the hammer, and why are you intent on beating the door frame?"

He laughed again, and kicked the toolbox closed. Metal clattered as the clasp engaged. "Over the years weather splintered the wood. Nora never bothered to lock her doors, but she figured you might feel differently. So she asked me to take care of it, and a few other things, before she...passed on." His voice lowered, and a hint of sadness shadowed his eyes.

"How did you know Aunt Nora? She never mentioned you. Why did she ask you to fix the door...and other things? Why—"

"Whoa. One bullet at a time." He held up a hand. "My grandparents were Nora's neighbors for years, and I helped her from time to time when I came out to visit. And then when I moved in year before last, Nora and I became friends and I began to help her more."

"Oh, wait a minute." Caroline ran a hand through damp hair, pacing. "She did mention you just before...she mentioned you might..." The floor blurred as tears filled her eyes.

"I'm sorry for your loss, Caroline. Nora was a beautiful soul. She's going to be sorely missed."

"I-I know. I'm sorry for...blubbering. I'm just very tired." Caroline's throat tightened. The sound of her name on his lips unnerved her. "If you don't mind leaving now—"

The thud of footsteps drew Caroline's attention to the doorway. "Uncle Matt, I found the hardware to fix the door in the basement, where you said it would be..." A boy Caroline guessed to be about fifteen, tall and lanky with huge blue eyes and coal-black hair, strode into the room. He took one look at Caroline and stopped in his tracks. "What's going on?"

His arms were splattered hand to elbow in what looked like white paint, and he was the spitting image of Matt-with-the-hammer, except leaner and lacking the muscle definition. Caroline guessed it would come with age.

"Paul, this is Caroline Lafollette and her daughter

Callie."

"Oh, you're from…

"Chicago." Caroline finished. "May I have that towel?"

Paul tossed her the tattered towel he'd balled in his hands. "Uncle Matt said you weren't coming 'til next week."

A flash of lightning rent the sky followed by a roar of thunder that rattled the house's front windows. Wind whistled through the hole in the front door. Callie whimpered and wiggled on the couch as rain gushed through the gutters to pool along the front yard.

"It's OK, honey." Caroline murmured and bent to kiss her forehead. "Mama's here."

Callie sat up and rubbed sleep from her pretty blue eyes. She yawned wide as the Pacific Ocean, then pressed a tiny hand to Caroline's cheek. "I'm hungry, Mama, an' thirsty."

"Me, too." Caroline sighed, and weariness settled in her bones. She rubbed a painful kink from her neck.

"I was going to stock the fridge for you…" Matt's voice trailed off.

"There's a cooler in my car, in the drive beside your truck." She lowered her gaze. "We…almost plowed into your truck, just before we ran out of gas."

"Mama." Callie yawned again and tugged the hem of Caroline's shirt. "My belly is rumblin'. Can I have some fruit snacks and juice?"

"Hop down and stretch your legs, sweetie." Matt glanced out the window. "The lightning's easing to the east, taking the angry clouds and downpour with it. In a few minutes I'll go get the cooler."

❧❧

The small cooler peeked just out of reach through the front passenger window, but it might as well have been miles away. The door was locked tight and a scuffed brown leather purse—Caroline's, Matt assumed—lay beside a set of car keys. He remembered Nora, and what she'd told him just before she passed.

"Caroline's been down a rough road, Matt. Her heart's been shattered. Help her get the house in order. Be patient."

He knew all about shattered hearts. There were plenty to go around. It was an epidemic.

Matt dodged light raindrops back to the house. Dawn bathed the pasture in a milky-pink halo.

Through the expanse of bay windows, he saw Caroline take a second towel from Paul. She rubbed the rain from her hair and stretched her back like a cat— long legs and torso topped with a mass of caramel curls.

Flannel looks good on her.

The thought startled Matt, and he switched gears fast. The last thing he needed was to get tangled up with a woman. But she'd surprised him by arriving early. She must have driven all night long. And all he got for his attempt to help her was a door slammed in his face and a broom jabbed at his belly.

Talk about a rough road…

He'd take her to his house, make sure she and the kid had something decent to eat before Caroline fell asleep on her feet. Dark smudges shadowing her eyes told the story…the woman was beyond exhausted.

Yeah, he'd make them both something to eat, and then send them on their way, grab a shower, and head to church. He had enough on his plate, dealing with his misguided sister and trying to keep Paul on the straight and narrow.

He'd honor Nora's wishes and help Caroline settle in here, that was all…that was enough.

2

"I'm going to have to take you home with me." Matt announced when he returned to the house.

"What?" Caroline's panicked honey eyes widened three sizes, making him laugh out loud.

"Relax. Your car's locked…and the cooler and your purse are held prisoner in the passenger seat."

"Oh. I guess I bumped the lock in my rush to get Callie. The wind was gusting, and the lightning…"

"No need to explain. It could happen to anyone."

"Don't you have a crowbar or something you can use to pry open the door?"

"Andie's dad can open it," Paul chimed in. "He's got special tools, being a police officer and all."

"They're not awake yet." Matt glanced out the window and saw the house beyond the pasture, kitty-corner to his, was still dark. "Maybe in an hour or so. We might as well get our bellies full while we wait."

"I don't want to trouble you." Caroline ran fingers through her hair to loosen the tangles. Damp waves cascaded over her shoulders and clung to her neck. An odd tug took root in Matt's gut and he shrugged his shoulders in an attempt to shake it off.

"It's no trouble." Matt studied the smudges beneath Caroline's eyes. "Besides, you look like you can use a good meal."

"Does this mean we can have pancakes?" Paul

asked. "Uncle Matt makes the best pancakes."

"Chocolate chip?" Callie piped up, crossing the room. "My daddy made the best chocolate chip pancakes."

My daddy...Matt's gut twisted. What kind of guy let his wife and daughter traipse across the country alone...and through the worst storms of the season, to boot?

"I can do chocolate chip." He nodded, patting Callie's head as she galloped over to stand beside him. "There's a break in the rain. Let's go."

❧❧

Sunlight bathed the breakfast table where Paul and Callie were seated. Paul had Callie's undivided attention while he sketched cartoons in a fat, wire-bound sketchbook. Wooden French doors opened onto an expansive deck and ushered in a warm breeze, clean with the scent of rain-washed earth.

"Your house is beautiful." Caroline ran a hand over a beige soapstone countertop. In the splendor of the morning sun, homey details came to light. A collection of ceramic pitchers lined the cabinet tops, and colorful nature stills, beautifully framed and matted, graced the walls. "How long have you lived here?"

"My grandfather built the house fifty-two years ago. When he and my grandmother retired to a golf community near Knoxville a few years ago, I decided to buy the house and property from them. The timing was...right, and there are a lot of memories here." The way he hesitated made Caroline wonder just what circumstances were included in that timing.

"But the house looks new."

"Yeah, that took some work." Matt grinned. "But an old house is like a buried treasure. You just have to know how to unearth it, Caroline."

"Like a treasure hunt. Right, Mama?" Callie squirmed in her seat and chair legs scraped against tile.

Caroline cringed at the thought of dingy white paint peeling from clapboard siding on the front of Aunt Nora's house. She'd noted a pair of shutters. Each dangled eerily from a single respective hinge, stinging the face of the old house like angry wasps with each gasp of breeze. And that was the least of her problems. But she plastered on a billboard grin and patted Callie's head. The last thing Callie needed was to see worry shadow her eyes. "Sure, honey. After breakfast we'll begin our own treasure hunt."

"But, Mama, it's Sunday." Callie glanced up from the sketch Paul added finishing details to. "Matt and Paul are getting ready to go to church. Matt said we can go with them, too. Can we, Mama?"

Caroline shook her head as a knot twisted in her belly. "Not today, Callie."

"You always say that, Mama." Callie's blue eyes widened. "I want to go."

"We can't. The house is waiting, and we need to get settled in. There's so much to do."

"But, Mama—"

"No." Caroline turned away from the table and crossed her arms. It was hard to deny the innocent longing in Callie's eyes. She lowered her voice. "And that's final."

Matt opened a cabinet beside the stove and pulled out a griddle. "Maybe next week," he offered. "By then you'll have had some time to brush off the cobwebs and settle in. But for now…pancakes and some strong coffee. It's not a good idea to go on a treasure hunt without the proper fuel."

"I don't like coffee." Callie's sweet voice fluttered across the kitchen. "At least I don't *think* so. Mama says it's a grown-up drink, so I've never had any. I like milk, though."

Matt laughed. "Chocolate or white?"

"Mmm…chocolate's my favorite!" She gave a little clap.

"I'll make you some." Paul took a pint of chocolate syrup from the refrigerator, found a glass in the cabinet to the left of the sink.

Caroline cringed. "I don't know…chocolate milk with chocolate chip pancakes? That's an awful lot of sugar for one meal."

"Relax, Caroline." Matt poured coffee into an oversized mug and handed it to her. "Why don't you sit and take a load off while I make you a short stack?"

"A short stack?"

"He means pancakes, Mama." Callie rolled her eyes. "Paul drew me a picture. See?" She took the sketch pad and turned it toward Caroline. A pile of pancakes sat on a platter, topped with a generous slab of butter and drizzled with syrup.

"Unless you'd rather have a tall stack," Matt's gaze swept her petite frame.

"I can draw that, too." Paul reached for the sketch pad. His charcoal pencil scratched along the paper.

"That's a whole tower of pancakes, Mama." Callie scrambled to her knees in the chair and peered over Paul's shoulder. "That's what I'm havin'."

Caroline sighed. "A short stack will be fine." She slid into a chair at the table beside Callie and glanced at the pancakes Paul sketched. "You draw very well, Paul. Have you taken classes?"

"No." He shrugged. "I just like to doodle."

"I'd call that more than doodling. May I see?" He nodded. She took the pad and flipped through it. On one page he'd rendered a flattering likeness of Callie, capturing the mischievous glow in her eyes to a *T.* "You've got a real talent."

"Thanks." The quick flash of a grin made his blue eyes shine. "Uncle Matt says so, too."

"Well, he's right."

"I can draw you if you'd like."

Caroline imagined the sight of her—tangled hair, mascara-smudged cheeks, sleep-shadowed eyes, and quickly shook her head. She handed the paper back to him. "Maybe some other time, OK?"

"Sure." Paul flipped to a clean page and turned his attention back to Callie. "What do you want me to draw now, munchkin?"

"A princess in a pretty dress." She clapped her hands again and bobbed in the chair. "With a crown, too—real sparkly."

Caroline shook her head as Paul blended smooth strokes. Callie'd boss him all day, if she had her way. The child was like a serious adult in a miniature body.

"I'll put a few gallons of gas in your car when we're done here." Matt dropped a pat of butter on the hot griddle and it sizzled and spat, filling the room with a mouth-watering aroma. The hunger in Caroline's belly roared to life. "We always have extra on hand for mowing and the generator, and that should be enough to get you into town for anything you may need."

"Thank you, Matt." She reached for her purse,

frowned when she remembered it was still locked in the car. "How much do I owe you?"

"Nothing, Caroline. It's what neighbors do."

She watched him pour batter onto the griddle and a melancholy longing swept over her. Sunday mornings used to be for pancakes with Curt, too, before they dressed for church and piled Callie into the car.

Caroline shook the memory from her mind. She gulped coffee, searing her throat. Curt was gone, taken in a senseless act of selfish rage, and no amount of longing would bring him back. It was best to move on...move forward.

"We'll just have some breakfast, and then Callie and I will be out of your way."

"Oh, you're not in the way at all." Matt flipped a quartet of nicely-browned pancakes. "You can have breakfast here anytime."

"No offense, but I hope I don't repeat the blunder of locking my keys in the car and imposing on you again."

He glanced up as he transferred the pancakes from the griddle to a platter already piled high with nicely-browned discs. "Then I'll just have to invite you back, do things properly."

Was he coming on to her? Surely not. She'd stumbled onto the doorstep during a raging thunderstorm and tried to skewer him with a push broom. He'd probably spend the next month laughing his head off with his buddies down at the corner store.

Caroline sipped the steaming coffee and felt her energy slowly recharge.

"Are you sure you won't come to church with us?" Matt set the platter of pancakes on the table and settled in beside her. Rich chocolate wafted up to greet her.

She nodded. "My hair is a tangled mess, and the bags under my eyes could hold a week's worth of groceries."

Matt studied her. "You look good to me."

"Yeah, well..." Caroline avoided the real issue...that she hadn't been inside a church in nearly a year. Oh, she still had her faith. But she couldn't bring herself to step foot inside the walls of a church building. The memory of Curt was so strong, the way his life was taken inside church walls still so fresh. Sometimes the pain took her breath away.

"Oh, Mama, please!" Callie begged. "I want to go!"

"No, Callie."

"But, Mama"

"I said, no. That's final. Now eat your pancakes so we can leave."

"Yes, Mama."

"Will you say grace, Paul?" Matt refilled Callie's glass with chocolate milk.

"I guess." He set his sketchbook aside and reached for Callie's hand.

Matt took Caroline's. Callouses on his palms brushed her skin, and her belly clenched. As Paul's voice filled the room, she stared at the pancakes drowning in syrup while her vision blurred with tears. Her appetite fled, and she could only stare at her food as the others dug in. Forks clinked against porcelain and Callie gulped milk. Caroline smoothed trembling hands across the thighs of her jeans, still damp from rushing through the rain. The memory of Curt's gentle touch filtered into her mind, and guilt pierced her heart. She shouldn't be reacting to Matt's hand on hers.

She felt like a traitor. Her foot tapped the tile floor, the soggy sock rubbing against her chilled toes. A tear slid down her cheek, and she swiped at it, sniffling, as Matt's gaze questioned.

"I...I'm sorry, Matt." She lowered her gaze. "I've lost my appetite."

"It's OK. You're exhausted. I'll wrap up a few pancakes and you can take them with you." He poured her a second cup of coffee. "Have some more of this. Maybe it will help. Then I'll walk you home and perform surgery on your car."

"OK."

"Can I come back an' see you again?" Callie asked, her puckered lips laced with chocolate crumbs. "You can make lots more pancakes, and Paul can draw me more pictures. I like the pictures he makes. They're funny an'—"

"Callie, that's enough," Caroline hushed, dabbing her eyes with her napkin. "We've taken up too much of Matt's and Paul's time already."

Matt leaned toward her to whisper. "You and your mom are welcome anytime, sweetie."

"OK." Callie stuffed a final bite of pancake into her mouth and squirmed from her chair. "C'mon, Mama. We gotta go. Our new house is waitin'."

Caroline shook her head wearily. "Thank you, Matt, for everything. I don't know how I'll ever repay you."

He dipped his head. "It's been my pleasure, Caroline."

3

Caroline sank to her knees on stained linoleum that barely passed as a kitchen floor. The strong, clean scent of bleach tickled her nose. During a full-on daylight tour of the house, she'd quickly realized the enormity of the task at hand. Since Aunt Nora's death the house had stood vacant. And before that, with Aunt Nora's illness, she'd had little energy to see to even the simplest of tasks; it showed in the dust and cobwebs that darkened every corner. It was going to take an act of God and a truckload of cleaning supplies to put this house in order.

There were structural issues as well. Besides the peeling exterior paint and broken shutters, rotted floor planks on the back deck were an accident waiting to happen.

Inside, the kitchen sink leaked, and the refrigerator motor shrieked like a launching rocket. And on top of it all, Caroline met a family of burrowing, furry rodents. She'd managed to trap one beneath an overturned garbage can, and it scratched the plastic, desperate for release.

So, she knelt amid the dirt, drips, scratching, and wailing, and blew a lock of stray hair from her eyes. She sighed. "Dear Lord, you're going to have to help me here. I can't do this alone. Show me where to begin and what to do. Make me strong, Lord. And if you would, please make the furry interloper under the trash can disappear. I know he's one of Your creatures, and I don't have the heart to kill him. But I can't tolerate him in this house, either." She paused. "And, Lord, I'd be grateful if the refrigerator quit howling. Amen."

"Mama," Callie came bounding into the kitchen, blonde ringlets bouncing merrily. Her cheeks were pink and splotchy from the cool late-winter air. "Look what I found in the yard!"

"What, honey?" *Oh, Lord, don't let it be a snake.*

"Look." She thrust a fluffy gray kitten with snowy-white front paws into Caroline's arms. "Can we keep him, Mama? Can we?"

"Let's see." Caroline stroked soft fur that smelled of hay and wild onions. The kitten mewled and nestled warmly against her. "He seems healthy, and he's not wearing a collar."

"He likes you, Mama. He's talkin' to you."

"Yes, he is." The rumble of his vocal motor tickled her ribs. "I think he'll make a nice addition to our family. What will you call him?"

Callie considered a moment, scratching her head. "Socks. That's a good name. Look at his feet."

"Socks is perfect." Caroline hoped he liked mice, and lots of them. "Why don't you give him a tour of the house while I clean the kitchen? Then we'll go to the grocery store to get some food."

"Can we play outside?"

"Sure. Just don't go near the pond across the pasture." Caroline handed Socks back to Callie. "Stay where I can see you."

"I will, Mama."

Well, that's one prayer answered...an adorable mouse-

chasing kitten.

Guilt nagged at Caroline as she swished the mop into sudsy water and continued scrubbing the kitchen floor. Did God care that she didn't go to church anymore? Would He still listen to her prayers? Surely He understood how she felt...losing Curt within the walls of their church. And He must know the pain that lingered, the heartache that filled her whenever she considered attending again.

She sang as she worked, segueing from one hymn to another. A hearty rendition of *Amazing Grace* chased the guilt away, and she glanced out the window to check on Callie, who skipped up and down the driveway with Socks bundled in her arms.

"Hello? Caroline?"

Startled, she dropped the mop and water splattered her tennis shoes. A hand over her heart eased the galloping as she rushed to the front door.

"Matt." He stood on the porch with a grocery sack in each arm. "What're you doing here?"

"Was that you singing?"

Her belly flip-flopped as he eased toward her. She brushed hair that had escaped from her ponytail out of her eyes. "I didn't know anyone was listening."

"You have a beautiful voice. I hope I'm not interrupting."

"Only my assault on the kitchen and believe me, I can use a break. I've been trying to put things in order. The house is a virtual battleground."

"In that case, you'll need some rations." He lowered his arms to give her a glimpse into the pair of brown bags. "I brought you the essentials... cookies, macaroni and cheese, bread—"

"And strawberries!" A quart of the crimson fruit

peeked through one of the bags, and she breathed in a sweet aroma that got the juices in her belly flowing. "Oh, I love strawberries, Matt."

"I did OK, then."

"You did great." She opened the screen door. "Come in, if you dare."

"Oh, I dare." He followed her into the kitchen and set the bags on the counter. "I see you're not wielding the blunt end of a broom this afternoon?"

"No, the mop is my weapon of choice." Heat crept up her neck. "I'm sorry about that, Matt. I was tired, and a little on edge from the long drive...and the storm..."

"It's OK." He grinned and his eyes smiled beneath waves of coffee hair. "I'm just glad we got it all sorted out."

"Yeah. Me, too. And thanks for fixing the front door lock. I wouldn't have been able to sleep tonight with it broken."

"Me, either...worrying about you alone. Not that we have much to worry about in the way of crime around here, but still..."

Caroline nodded. That was one of the reasons she'd chosen Mountainview. "I'd offer you a seat, but, as you can see, I've been cleaning out the cabinets and trying to get things in some sort of order."

The tabletop was covered with plastic food savers and pot and pans, and each chair held a stack of plates or an army of glasses or stainless-steel mixing bowls.

"No problem." He went to the refrigerator, dropped to his knees, and peered beneath the dusty grate. "You've got some dirt clogging the compressor. Hand me a wet paper towel."

Caroline tore a couple from a roll on the counter

and ran water over them before handing them to Matt. He removed the grill and gave the motor a few swipes. The room became blissfully quiet.

Caroline planted her hands on her hips and gaped. "How did you do that?"

"I dunno. I just wiped things off." He shrugged. "It's no big deal."

"It is to me. Thank you."

He wadded the soiled towels. "Where's your trashcan?"

"Covering a disgusting rat." She grimaced and pointed to the back-porch doorway as she tapped a foot.

Matt loped over. He lifted the can a crack and peeked beneath, then burst into laughter. "It's just a field mouse, Caroline. It's more scared of you than you are of it."

Caroline scooted back, putting ample space between her and the beady-eyed intruder. "I highly doubt that."

Matt scooped the mouse into the trashcan and opened the back door. "I'll set some traps for you."

"Uh-uh." She shook her head. "I couldn't kill them."

"OK...but..." He turned the trashcan over and the mouse scurried across the yard. "They'll just keep coming back. Where's Callie?"

"Around the side of the house, with Socks."

"Socks?"

"The answer to our mouse problem. He's better than traps. Come look."

Matt peered out the window. "Oh, I see." Callie pushed her doll stroller through the grass as she chattered to the kitten. "You're right. He's probably a stray barn cat that wandered through the pasture. He'll scare the mice away."

"I hope so."

"I have to go to my truck for a minute. I'll be right back."

While he was gone, Caroline sorted through the grocery sacks. Her belly rumbled again at the sight of peanut butter and grape jam, a gallon of skim milk, apples, and fat, juicy-green grapes, a giant chocolate bar, and—God bless Matt—a pound of coffee. She searched the pantry shelves for a coffeemaker, found one tucked behind rows of outdated canned peaches, and rinsed it off. The aroma of fresh brew filled the kitchen by the time Matt strode back in wielding an oversized wrench.

"What are you planning to do with *that*?"

"Fix the leak in the sink. The coupling just needs to be tightened."

Caroline froze. Her prayers were answered. The refrigerator, the sink—the mice.

"Caroline, are you OK?"

"Um...yeah." She busied herself finding two mugs in the cabinet over the sink and washing a layer of dust off them. "How about some coffee?"

"That would be great."

She filled the mugs, handed him one. "Let's sit in the backyard. I love the view. The mountains are so beautiful." The air was resplendent with the scent of wild onions and jonquils that poked through soil along the deck. "I can't seem to get used to looking at them, like sentinels standing guard over the pasture."

"Nice analogy." Matt followed her onto the deck, and they carefully sidestepped rotting planks to settle in a safe spot at the rail. "So you don't miss the city?"

"No." The reply came so quickly, so forcefully, she felt compelled to elaborate. "What's there to miss? Concrete and traffic jams? Stuffy high-rise apartments? Noise and smog?"

The crime...memories of Curt?

She shook her head. "No, I don't miss it."

He propped a hip against the porch rail and sipped coffee. "You really have a lot of space here, especially if it's just you and Callie."

The comment caught her off guard. Was he testing the waters? He had a way of making her feel off-kilter. "Don't forget Socks."

"Oh, right."

"Our apartment back in the city was a fraction of the size of this house. And, of course, there was no yard. That's one of the reasons I moved here, to give Callie more room to grow. If only the house wasn't in such poor condition..."

"It's really not so bad, Caroline...kind of like a buried treasure that just needs to be dusted off and polished a little. I can help with that. I know my way around fixing things."

She saw that in his hands...so much larger than hers, and calloused yet gentle. She imagined them coaxing power tools and lumber into something beautiful. "I appreciate the offer, but it's my responsibility. I wouldn't dream of burdening you."

"It's no burden." Matt leaned back and stretched his powerful legs. "Coffee's good."

"Thanks for bringing it."

"I've kept you from your work long enough. I should go." His gaze swept the decaying deck, and he nodded as if making a mental note. "I'll be back soon to get started on things."

"No, really, Matt. That's not necessary." Caroline sipped her coffee, felt the slight jolt as caffeine kicked in. "Thank you for fixing my refrigerator and sink, and for taking care of the rat—"

"Field mouse."

"If you say so. And thanks for the food. Callie and I will enjoy peanut butter and jelly sandwiches with strawberries for dinner."

He finished his coffee and went back into the house, placing the mug in the kitchen sink. "Take this, Caroline." He handed her a slip of paper. The brush of his fingers against hers was innocent, yet it sparked a longing she thought she'd buried with Curt. She wondered if Matt could hear her heart pounding.

"What is it?"

"My cell number. Call me if you need anything, OK?"

4

Callie skipped into the room. "What are you doin', Mama?"

"Seeing what we need to do to get your bedroom in order. I don't want you to spend too many more nights sleeping on the hard floor." If only Curt had left an insurance policy, she wouldn't have had to sell so much of their furniture for travel money. The only pieces she'd kept belonged to Callie's bedroom set...it would give her a sense of home in a faraway place. And she'd donated her bed—Curt's bed—to the church where he'd lost his life. It just seemed fitting. "Besides, the moving van will be here tonight, and I'd like to have your room clean before they put the furniture in. Now, let's see...we'll need some paint for the walls. What color would you like?"

"Pink. And can I have some pictures, too?"

"You mean posters?"

"No. I mean pictures painted on the walls the way Felicia has."

"Felicia's mom is an artist, honey."

"You can be an artist, too, can't you, Mama?"

Caroline sighed and scanned the room. It did look awfully bare, and could certainly use a little pick-me-up. "I'll see what I can do. In the meantime, we'll need some throw rugs to cover this wood floor and a few shelves for your toys." She stepped to the window and fanned the curtains. Dust motes drifted through the air.

"New curtains aren't a bad idea, either."

Callie sneezed. "We need to clean, Mama. My nose itches."

"Yes. That's first on the list. Help me get these curtains down. Then we'd better mop the floor before the moving van arrives. I don't want to put your furniture on this dusty wood."

They made quick work of it, and soon had the room in order. Caroline surveyed the gleaming floor and a sparkling window that afforded a view of the Smoky Mountains in the distance.

"We'll go into town later this week and find a store that sells home goods, OK?"

"Yeah. But I'm hungry now, Mama. Is it lunchtime yet?"

She checked her watch. "Oh, my. Where did the morning go? Let's head down to the kitchen and see what we can scrounge up. Bring Socks, too. Matt brought a few cans of tuna with the groceries on Sunday. I think Socks will settle for that until we can get to the store."

Callie grabbed the cat and followed her down the stairs. "Can we sit outside on the front porch?"

"I think that's a wonderful idea." Caroline scooped tuna into a bowl for Socks, who prowled around her ankles, purring. "We'll have a picnic."

"I like it here." Callie said. "I can run around and be wild, like Max in *Where the Wild Things Are.*"

"Should I send you to bed without any supper?"

"Oh, no, Mama." Her eyes widened as she shook her head. "I'd be way too hungry. I don't like that part of the story at all."

Caroline tapped her nose. "But, what if supper was spinach and broccoli?"

"Well, maybe then it would be OK. But I wouldn't want you to be mad like Max's mama."

"I love you." Caroline hugged Callie and inhaled the scent of apple shampoo that clung to her pretty blonde curls.

"I love you, too, Mama."

Moments later, they nibbled turkey sandwiches and fat strawberries.

"When can I start school here, Mama?"

"Tomorrow. You're all registered and ready to go." It had been a difficult decision for Caroline to resign from her job and pull Callie from her grammar school so late in the year, but all things considered, it was for the best.

"Do you think I'm gonna like it?"

"You're going to love it, honey. And the teachers will love you, too." Caroline leaned against the porch rail and sipped coffee. "And remember, if you need anything I'll be right across the street three days a week, at Mountainview High School."

"Being a guidance counselor, right?"

"That's right." The position would be a welcome relief from the emotional stress of dealing with the struggling addicts at her previous job.

"And when will you start school, Mama?"

"Next Monday." Caroline wished she could work at the school full-time, but the position was merely part-time for now. She'd just have to be patient and see what happened. "In the meantime, I'll be here, working on getting this silly old house in order. The school's just ten minutes away, so I can be there in a jiffy if you need me."

"But, what if you get lost?"

"I used to spend summers here with Aunt Nora,

so I pretty-much know where things are. But if it will help you feel better, we'll make a practice run later. Then we won't have to worry about getting lost, OK?"

"OK, Mama. I like that idea. Look! There's the moving van."

Gravel crunched as the truck wound up the drive. Caroline waved a greeting, relieved the driver had found the house.

"You stay close while I show the workers where everything goes, OK?"

"I'll show them, too!"

Callie's twin bed and dresser fit nicely into her room, allowing plenty of play area, and the entrance hall had a narrow oak table that Caroline could toss her purse on when she came home from a day at work. A pair of lamps on the living room end tables rounded things out. "It looks like home, now, Mama."

"Except for that stack of boxes pushed against the living room wall, filled with clothes and toys. I'll have to empty each one and put everything away tomorrow."

"Where's your bed?" Callie searched the room as if the four-poster might magically appear.

"I donated it to the church just before we left. They can sell it at their annual yard sale to raise money for missions. I thought I'd get a new bed."

"Why, Mama? Didn't you like it?"

How could she explain to the child that she could no longer bear to sleep in the bed she'd shared with Curt before he died? She patted Callie's head. "It was just time, honey. Now, go check on Socks. He's probably not used to having so many people around. He might be frightened."

When the movers left, Caroline showered off

layers of grime and changed into fresh jeans and a white peasant blouse. By the time she finished applying a touch of blush and a hint of lip gloss, she felt almost human again.

"Callie, where are you, honey?" She worked the kinks from her spine and made her way to the living room.

"Out here, Mama, on the porch."

She found Callie perched on the front steps, Socks cradled in her lap. Matt sat beside her, dressed in Levi's and a navy blue T-shirt that hugged well-formed muscles. Caroline ran a hand through her tousled, damp hair as his blue eyes swept over her.

"Matt brought me a present, Mama. He made it himself." Callie held up a wooden plaque, brightly painted and bearing her name in neat, carved block letters.

"Wow, that's nice." Caroline ran a finger over the smooth wood. "We'll find a special place for it in your bedroom."

Matt cleared his throat and stood to face her. "Hi, Caroline."

"Hello, Matt." She felt an odd constriction in her chest. He looked so...masculine, and the clean scent of soap clung to his skin. "When did you get here?"

"A few minutes ago. Callie's been entertaining me with details of your day. It sounds like you've had quite an adventure."

"If you call mopping and dusting and moving furniture an adventure, we've had plenty."

"Matt came to check on us. Isn't that nice?" Callie loosened her hold on Socks, and he pounced from her lap to prowl the yard.

"Yes, it is."

"I told him we're gonna drive to my new school. We don't wanna get lost tomorrow, 'cause it's my first day and everything." She leaned in and whispered to Matt as he bent to listen, "I'm in first grade, you know."

"Really?" His eyes sparkled as her breath tickled his ear. "That's a pretty important grade."

"Yeah. We don't have time for a nap like in kindergarten. That was *so* boring." There was that eye-roll again. "And I get to read lots and lots of books. I like to read."

"I'll bet you're a great reader," Matt winked and straightened once more.

"Mama says I am."

"Well, your mom should know."

"Yeah. She's gonna be a guidance counselor at the high school three days a week, so she knows just about everything."

That scored a huge grin. "Really?"

"Uh huh. And the high school's right by my grammar school, so she can be there in a jiffy if I need her, and—"

"Callie, take a breath," Caroline said.

"But I don't need a breath, Mama."

"Well, maybe Matt's ears need a rest."

"My ears are just fine, Caroline." He tapped Callie's nose. "I like your stories, sweetie."

"Thank you." She smiled and ran after Socks, who'd burrowed beneath the azalea bushes beside the front stairs. "Can Matt come with us to see my school? I bet he'd like it lots."

"I'm sure Matt has other things he needs to do."

"Actually, I'm headed that way. I need to pick up a few groceries, and stop at the home improvement store for some paint for your living room. We can ride together, and you can choose the color you like. We can swing by the grammar school, too."

"We need to go, Mama. We need paint for my room, and rugs. And curtains. You said so. And we need food for Socks so he doesn't starve. And—"

"Callie, please." Caroline sighed and ran a hand through her hair.

"I'll drive." Matt grinned. "We can't deny Socks a square meal, now, can we?"

"Just let me grab my purse...and Callie's booster seat."

~∞~

"Thank you for getting us into the grammar school for a tour, Matt. It meant the world to Callie. Principal Jenner is so kind."

"Marian Jenner and I have gone to church together for years. She's a dedicated principal. You'll be pleased with Callie's quality of education."

"I liked the library," Callie chimed in. "There's lots and lots of books. Can we read them all, Mama?"

"Sure, a few at a time."

"And Principal Jenner said there's a cafeteria, so I don't need to bring lunch. Tuesday is Chicken Nugget Day. Yum!"

"Speaking of food, I think we need to fortify ourselves before heading to the shopping center. I got a glimpse of your list, Caroline, and we may be there a while. What's Callie's favorite food?"

"Pizza!" Callie shouted.

"I can manage that. There's a pizza place in the shopping complex."

Two hours later they'd finished their meal and completed the rounds at the store. Caroline's purchases filled two shopping carts and overflowed into a third.

"It's a good thing you have a truck," she said as they loaded the bags into the extended bed.

"It's good for hauling building supplies." Matt unlocked the door and helped Callie into her booster seat in the rear of the crew cab. "You look tired, sweetie."

"My eyes are sleepy." Callie yawned and stretched. "Mama, when are you gonna paint my room?"

"Maybe tomorrow while you're at school. We'll see."

"You don't have to work?" Matt asked.

"No. I start next Monday. It's a good thing, too. It may take me that long to put all this stuff away." And their savings would last just a bit longer— if the ancient water heater and gasping furnace held out. At least the house was paid for— no more rent to worry about.

"Mama's gonna paint my room pink, and then she's gonna draw pictures on the walls and color them, too. Like a princess and a castle."

"Callie," Caroline frowned. "I told you I'm not an artist. You'll just have to settle for some posters instead."

"But, Mama—"

"Hush. We'll discuss it later."

"OK, Mama." She rubbed her eyes and settled back in the seat. "But I really want pictures."

"I know you do, honey."

Matt eased the truck into gear and headed toward home. "So, you're a counselor?"

Caroline nodded. "I was offered a part-time position at the high school. It's a foot in the door, and if it works out it may turn into full-time next year."

"I hope it works out, then."

"Me, too. The counselor I'm filling in for, Jill Rothgeb, is going on maternity leave. Maybe she'll enjoy staying home so much she'll decide to make it permanent."

"Oh, I know Jill and her husband, Tony. He works on the police force with Kevin." Matt nodded.

"Kevin's my neighbor—the police officer who unlocked my car Sunday morning?"

"Yeah, and, given Tony's erratic schedule, I wouldn't be surprised if Jill made the leave permanent. Sure would be a lot easier to take care of the baby that way."

They turned onto Collier Road and Caroline's house came into view.

"Oh, look at that gorgeous sunset." Hues of bubblegum-pink and brilliant magenta played hide-and-seek with the white frame house and rounded peaks of the Smokies beyond.

"It's a beauty. Gonna be a clear night...lots of stars. Paul will probably have his telescope out when I get home. I'll have to drag him inside to do homework."

"Sunsets like this were virtually non-existent in the city, with all the streetlights and smog. I forgot how beautiful they are."

Matt pulled up the drive and parked in front of the house. Callie had fallen asleep in the booster seat, and she snored softly.

"You don't have to wake her," Matt said as Caroline slipped from her seat and unlatched the rear door. "I'll carry her in for you."

"That would be great. Thanks." Caroline's back screamed from scrubbing floors and moving furniture, and Matt's help was a welcome relief. "I'll follow you in." She watched as Matt gathered Callie into his arms. "Her room's at the top of the stairs. Take her up there, if you don't mind, and I'll follow you to tuck her in. She'll probably just sleep straight through the night. All the excitement has finally caught up with her."

"You've got a sweet daughter, Caroline. You're an amazing mom to do this on your own. I know it's not easy."

"It helps to pray a lot. I've certainly had more than my fair share of conversations with God."

"Ditto."

Matt's shoes brushed the scuffed stairs as they made their way to the second floor. Aging wood creaked beneath every footstep. Caroline switched on a nightlight as he placed Callie in the bed. "Where's her father?"

"He's..." She gazed out the bedroom window, across the darkening pasture, to where Matt's house sat like a sturdy sentinel shadowed by sleeping mountains beyond. "Um..."

"You don't have to answer. I shouldn't have asked."

Caroline crossed her arms and shook her head with a single tight jerk. "He's dead...murdered."

Matt's voice softened and she felt the brush of his hand on her shoulder. "Oh, Caroline...that's horrible. I'm sorry."

She turned to him, and her throat clenched with the threat of tears. "Curt was a good man. And he gave me Callie. For that, I will be eternally grateful. But I came here because the grief was killing me, and it's time…to move on."

"I understand. Believe me, I do. It's going to be OK, Caroline."

She pressed a hand to her mouth. "You think so?"

"Yes, I do." He hesitated, then brushed a stray curl from her cheek. "I'll unload the truck while you tuck Callie in."

When he left she snugged the blankets around Callie's shoulders and brushed matted curls back to kiss her forehead. The screen door slapped against its frame as Matt returned from the truck to drop packages on the living room floor below. Caroline closed the window drapes and brushed hot tears from her cheeks before hurrying down to help.

When everything was safely inside the house, Caroline turned to Matt. "Would you like a cup of coffee or a soda before you go?"

"I would, but I really should get home and check on Paul. There's no telling what he might be into."

"OK." She caught her lower lip between her teeth and bit down as she thought of the dark, lonely night ahead.

"Do you want me to help you put this stuff away?"

Caroline shook her head. "I can manage things from here. Thank you so much, Matt. I really appreciate everything you've done to help me and Callie."

"My pleasure." He stepped onto the porch, illuminated by security lights. He paused and turned to face her. "Caroline, are you busy Friday evening?"

Her heart did an odd little dance. "Hmmm...unless you consider cleaning and painting busy, no."

"Would you like to come to my place for dinner? I

could toss a few steaks on the grill."

"Steak…mmm, I'd love to."

"Six-thirty OK?"

"Perfect."

"Great. I'll see you then." He dipped his head to her, a gentleman's bow.

"Goodnight, Matt."

"Goodnight, Caroline. Sleep well."

❧

"What are you doing out here?" Paul settled into a rocking chair on the back porch beside Matt.

"I should ask you the same." Matt sipped from a glass of sweet tea. It was good, but not as good as the sun tea Nora used to make for him when he stopped by her place to fix a broken pipe or leaky toilet. "It's late. You should be in bed."

"I couldn't sleep."

"Thinking about girls?" Matt paused, waited. Beside him, Paul's knee bounced like a piston. The scent of lilacs and hay from the pasture beyond washed over them as crickets serenaded beneath a starlit sky.

Paul cleared his throat. "Yeah. How did you know?"

"They're hard to figure out, that's for sure."

"You mean it doesn't get any easier?"

Matt laughed softly, drew another sip of the tea. "You have no idea."

"You got home pretty late tonight." Paul's dark gaze glittered like a prowling tiger's. "Where were you?"

"I helped Caroline pick up some things for her

42

house. She's coming to dinner Friday evening."

"Good. It's about time you have someone over. A *woman*, I mean.

"Since when are you concerned about my social life?"

"Since...I don't know." He picked a piece of lint from his jeans. "You must be lonely since Aunt Mandy...well...you know."

"You can say it, Paul."

"I don't want to upset you."

Matt sighed. "The manager from Bartlett's Grocery Store called. You need to call him back. The number's on the fridge. What's that all about?"

"I filled out a work application. They're hiring baggers."

"That's a job you can do."

"Yeah. And I won't have to bug you for a ride, 'cause I can take my bike 'til I get my license."

"Hard to believe you'll turn sixteen in June."

"Yeah. I can't wait."

Ah, to be young again...and innocent. Matt quickly put the brakes on that line of thinking. Paul wasn't innocent. He'd seen too much in his young life to be innocent. But he was on the right track, on a good road now, and Matt hoped he stayed there. Time would tell.

"You should get some sleep. Don't you have an algebra test tomorrow?"

"Thanks for reminding me."

"By the way, your mom left a message on the answering machine. Call her tomorrow."

Anger flared in an instant, and Paul was suddenly on his feet, pacing the length of the porch. "Why should I call her? I don't have anything to say."

"Look, your mom's trying to make things right, Paul. You need to try, too. The rehab's going better than expected, and she found a job answering phones in a warehouse office. Call her tomorrow." His tone left no room for discussion.

"Yeah, whatever." Paul slapped the thighs of his jeans. "I've gotta study. G'night, Uncle Matt." The rocking chair clattered as he pushed past and stomped into the house, letting the screen door slap behind him.

Matt grimaced. He settled back in the chair and willed his blood pressure to return to normal. His gaze was drawn to the flicker of lights in the house across the pasture. For the first time in months, memories of Mandy weren't foremost in his mind. Instead, the scent of Caroline's honeysuckle shampoo washed over him, and her easy smile filled his senses.

He pulled his worn, brown leather billfold from the back pocket of his jeans and flipped it open to find the photograph of Mandy he'd taken two winters ago. She smiled into the camera, one hand splayed across the mound of her belly. He remembered that day clearly, how they'd gone to pick up furniture for the nursery. He'd spent the afternoon putting a crib and changing table together, then watched her tuck impossibly tiny booties and gowns into drawers. Though exhausted, she'd beamed as he'd snapped the photo of her standing beside the crib that was draped in soft pink pastels and smiling teddy bears. Who knew she'd be gone in a matter of days?

Matt removed the picture from its plastic casing and brushed his lips across the image. Then he tucked the photo into his pocket and closed the wallet. Tomorrow he'd take down the few framed portraits scattered around the living room and find a safe place to store them.

Caroline was right about moving on. It was time.

5

With a final swipe, Caroline finished the second coat of bubblegum-pink paint. As she stepped back to admire her handiwork, the roar of an engine in the yard startled her. The roller she used to slap color on Callie's bedroom walls slipped, leaving a smear across one cheek that was reflected in Callie's dresser mirror. She dropped the roller into a pan and rushed to the window to see Matt climb onto a riding mower.

She threw open the window and leaned out to shout over the mower's growl. "What in the world are you doing?"

Matt grinned up at her. "Weather's beginning to warm, so I thought I'd better tame the jungle in your front yard."

"But you spent most of the day yesterday painting my living room."

"Looks good, too, doesn't it?"

"You're doing too much, Matt. At this rate, I'll never be able to repay you."

Matt backed the mower off a trailer attached to the back of his truck. "Go back to your painting, Caroline. Pink looks good on you."

"You're impossible!" She dismissed him with a wave of her hand to slip back into the room. But the window remained open, allowing a gentle breeze to freshen the air. She climbed the stepladder Matt had left for her when he'd finished the living room yesterday, and, since the walls were done, she carefully brushed crisp, white paint over thick crown molding along the ceiling.

Outside, the mower made rounds in the yard. The hum of the engine soothed Caroline's raw nerves, and she began to sing. She hardly noticed when the mower's engine died. The sound of footsteps creaking on the stairs outside Callie's room told her Matt was coming up.

"Looks good."

"Thanks." Caroline turned to find him leaning in the doorway. The scent of freshly-mown grass and an undertone of something spicy, purely masculine, wafted on the breeze that swirled through the bedroom window. A few lawn clippings clung to Matt's faded jeans.

"I love your singing."

"Caught me again." Blush warmed her face. She turned away and studied the crown molding. "I was just checking to see if I missed any spots."

"Looks good to me. You paint real well, Caroline. The color is..."

"Bright, huh?" She stepped down from the ladder. "But Callie likes it, and I guess that's what matters."

"It'll grow on you."

"I hope so." She wiped her hands on a towel. "Would you like some lemonade?"

"That sounds good. It's warming up out there." He swiped a forearm across his brow. "Spring'll be here before you know it."

"The breeze is nice. It'll help air out the room." She untied the bandanna that covered her head and released her hair from an elastic band so it tumbled down her back. "I thought about taking a walk down to the pond before I pick up Callie from school. Would you like to come?"

"Sure. I have some time before I have to meet a client about a project."

"What do you do?" Caroline started down the stairs. "I mean, for a living?"

"I remodel houses. I like getting my hands dirty. It's oddly gratifying."

"I could analyze that." She smirked over her shoulder. "But I'll refrain."

"Thanks." He gave her a lopsided grin. "I appreciate your restraint."

In the kitchen, Caroline poured the lemonade. They drained tall plastic tumblers before heading out the back door and crossing the pasture to the pond. A gentle breeze carried the scent of lilac bushes that were just coming into bloom along the fence row.

"I can't believe all this beautiful, open space belongs to me now." Caroline paused to gaze across the expanse of pasture. Sunshine warmed her face. "What was Aunt Nora thinking, leaving me all this?"

"Maybe she knew you needed a change, a new beginning." Matt studied her, and she brushed a finger against her cheek to feel a dried smudge of paint.

"I'm not one to run from my problems...but I guess I gave in this time, to some extent."

"Oh, I don't think you're running." Matt shook his head. "You're a brave woman, Caroline."

"You hardly know me." She shrugged. "Maybe I'm just a big wimp."

He laughed softly. "Fiercely independent, yes. A wimp, no."

"Thank you for mowing my lawn...and for the

fresh paint in my living room. You seem to have a lot of surprises up your sleeve."

"All good ones, I hope." He smoothed a stray hair from her cheek with a brush of his knuckles. "That shade of pink really compliments your eyes."

She swiped her face and grimaced. "I'm a mess. I'll bet I have paint in my hair, too."

"Just a little."

The heat of his gaze, coupled with the warmth of the sun, made Caroline feel as if she were melting. She took a deep breath, filled her lungs with the scent of wild onions and horses grazing in the pasture over the hill.

"Do you think having a pond on the property should worry me?" She gnawed her lower lip.

"What do you mean?"

"Callie's fascinated by the water. She chased Socks down here yesterday, too."

"Well, it's not very deep, except after a heavy rain. I'm sure she could touch the bottom, but even still..."

"I'm just not used to this particular kind of worry. Traffic...crossing the street...strangers and all that, yes. But a pond and an inquisitive kid...not so much."

"Does she know how to swim?"

"No. She was about to start lessons at the YMCA, but then we moved away."

"If you're that worried, Caroline, I'd be glad to teach her."

"Thanks." She shook her head. "But you don't have to do that. I'm just being overprotective." She shrugged then added, "Maybe I can enroll her in a program this summer."

"The community center has a swim program. I'll pick up some information the next time I'm out there."

"Thanks, Matt. That's very kind of you. I should hurry back to the house. I have to get Callie from school soon."

"I'll walk you back," he offered. "And I'll see you on Friday, then?"

"Friday?"

"For dinner, remember? Steak and baked potatoes with a few ears of corn-on-the-cob thrown in for good measure, maybe a little time on the porch swing afterwards, and a walk in the moonlight?"

"Oh, dinner. Right." Her stomach did a funny little flip.

A porch swing...moonlight?

❧

"Do you like your new room?" Caroline asked Callie as she tucked her into bed that night.

"I love it, Mama. It's so pretty." Callie rolled over in the twin bed and gazed out the window that Caroline had left open a crack to help clear the odor of paint. "But I'd really like some pictures on the walls."

"I know. I'll work on that, honey."

"Where are you gonna sleep, Mama? You don't have a bed yet."

"I ordered one. It should arrive in a few days. But the couch is comfortable enough, for now."

Callie sighed, her sweet face drawn tight with thought. "Do you miss Daddy?"

"Yes. You?" Caroline kept her tone light, though the question knotted her belly.

"Uh huh." Callie's head bobbed against the pillow. "Sometimes I dream about him. Do you dream about him too, Mama?"

Caroline's voice caught. "Sometimes, honey." She brushed Callie's soft hair from her brow and kissed the apple scent. "Yes, I do."

&

"Hi, Caroline." Matt took the cake platter from her as she and Callie entered his house Friday evening. "What's this? It smells delicious."

"Strawberry shortcake. I found the recipe in Aunt Nora's file."

"I helped make it." Callie informed him as she rocked on her heels. "I got to crack the eggs and stir the batter and everything."

"Is that so? In that case, I can't wait to have a huge slice."

"You've gotta eat your dinner first, though. That's Mama's rule. I don't like it, especially when there's lima beans. *Yuck.* But Mama says a rule's a rule, and you have to follow it anyway."

"Well, I sure don't want to break your mama's rule."

"No, you don't." Callie gazed at him, wide-eyed. "You didn't make lima beans, did you?"

"No." He shook his head. "No way. I don't like them, either."

"Whew, good!" Callie grinned and went on. "Look, I brought my sketchpad for Paul to draw some pictures in. It's brand new. Mama bought it for me today when we went to the mall. She needed some new lipstick and a pretty shirt."

Matt's gaze grazed Caroline's peach blouse, then her lightly-glossed, berry lips. "Hmmm, nice. That shade looks good on you, Caroline."

"Thank you." Heat swam across her cheeks as he turned his attention back to Callie.

"Let me see your sketch pad." Matt bent to her level. "It's very nice."

"I want to be an artist when I grow up, so I can draw pictures for books. Mama says drawing like that is a lot of hard work, but I can do it if I really want to."

"I think that's an admirable goal. Paul's out on the back porch with his friend, Andie. Why don't you show him your sketchpad? I'm sure he'd like to see it."

"OK." When she skipped away, humming, Matt reached into the cabinet and handed a glass to Caroline.

"How was your day?"

"Hectic, but satisfying." She leaned against the counter while he filled her glass with sweet tea and added a healthy lemon wedge. "I managed to put Callie's bookcases together and get all her picture books put away. Then I tackled the living room. I'm no expert on interior design, but the house is beginning to take on a comfortable feel. I'm starting to think of it as home."

"That's good to know. I like having you here. You begin work at the high school Monday?"

"Yes, and I have to admit I'm a little nervous about it. New school, new responsibilities. Plus, I don't know a soul there."

"I'm sure you'll do just fine. After all, look at Callie."

"She's blossomed under Marian's watchful eye. What an answer to my prayers!"

"Speaking of prayers, we're having a potluck lunch at the church this Sunday. I was wondering if you and Callie would like to come. It would give you a chance to get to know some people in the community. And Callie might make a new friend or two."

"I don't know..." She couldn't bring herself to tell him she hadn't stepped inside a church since Curt's funeral, and that she couldn't seem to get past the sense of betrayal that still lingered like an unwelcome stranger. "It's not that I don't want to go with you. I do. It's just..." She didn't belong in church any longer. Not after the hateful words and bitter thoughts she'd vented in a moment of rage following Curt's murder.

The memory shamed her, yet she still couldn't help pinning the blame where she was convinced it belonged. The security door should have been fixed. They told Curt it was fixed.

After her outburst, she no longer felt worthy—or safe—inside a church. At home, in her own quiet place, she could focus on God, could pray without distraction. But in church, her mind wandered to that night...to Curt, and resentment rushed in, blocking all other thought. How could she make Matt understand?

"You don't have to answer now," his voice coaxed. "Just think about it, OK?"

"OK." She could do that much, at least.

"Let's head out back and see what the kids are into. I'll toss a few steaks on the grill."

"Sounds like a plan."

When they stepped onto the deck, Paul stood from an Adirondack chair to greet her. "Hi, Caroline."

"Hello, Paul. It's good to see you again." She turned her attention to the dark-haired beauty with aquamarine eyes sitting beside him. "Who's this?"

"My..." He hesitated on the next word and she sensed it held more meaning. "...friend Andie. We go to school together."

Caroline offered a hand. "Pleased to meet you, Andie."

The girl smiled, nodded. "You moved into Nora's house?"

"That's right."

"We're neighbors, then. My dad helped you with your car."

"Oh, Kevin." Caroline nodded. "Yes."

Callie wiggled between them. "Mama, Andie rides horses really good."

"Really well, you mean," Caroline corrected.

"Really well." Callie echoed. "And she said she can teach me how. Can she, Mama? I'd like to ride."

Caroline's gaze swept from Callie to Andie, then back again as she considered the request. "We'll see."

Callie jumped up and down, clapping. "That means yes, Andie. When can we start?"

"Callie, I did not say yes," Caroline corrected firmly. "I meant I'd think about it."

"Don't you like horses, Mama?"

"Not much. I had a fall when I was about your age and broke my arm." She rubbed her elbow, remembering the sting as her bone snapped. "It hurt."

"I'm very careful," Andie assured her. "And I'm teaching Paul to ride. Believe me, if he can learn, anyone can. He used to be terrified of horses. When he first moved here, he wouldn't get *near* one, let alone *on* one."

"It's true," Matt confirmed. "Paul went off in a sulk during the pitch black of night. He stumbled into a pond on the Aronson's property. Andie heard him hollering for help, and she rode out to drag him from the water."

Caroline cringed. *He fell into the pond.*

Matt seemed to read her mind. "The Aronson's pond is much larger than yours, Caroline."

"Oh, well…"

"I threw him on my horse and carried him home," Andie continued.

"Quit exaggerating." Paul rolled his eyes. "That's not exactly how it happened."

"Close enough," Andie raised a hand to silence him. "It was cold that night, and Paul nearly drowned in the sweatshirt and jeans he was wearing. We never did find his shoes. He must have kicked them off while he was freaking out, trying haul himself out of the water."

"It was deep, and the sides were slick with mud. I couldn't get a foothold."

Matt leaned in. "That should teach you to go stomping off in the dark."

"Wow, Andie, you're a superhero." Callie's eyes grew huge as baseballs. "Maybe one day you'll rescue me like that."

"Let's hope that's never necessary." Caroline shuddered and wagged a finger at her. "You stay away from the pond, young lady. OK?"

"You're mama's right," Matt emphasized. "Some of the ponds around here are deep, and they can be dangerous. Don't wander near the one in your yard unless your mom's with you."

"OK." Callie's head bobbed.. "I won't. I promise."

"OK, then, let's dig into some steaks." Matt took them from the grill, heaping the meat onto an oversized platter. "Who wants to say grace?"

"I will!" Callie's hand shot up as she jumped up and down. "Pick me! Pick me!"

"Callie it is. Let's head for the table."

When they were settled, Matt reached for Caroline's hand on one side and Callie's on the other and bowed his head.

"Dear God," Callie's sweet voice filled the room. "Thank you for the yummy steaks and for our new friends. Bless everyone, especially my mama and Matt. And bless Daddy in Heaven. Amen."

"Amen." Caroline choked on tears. Matt squeezed her hand as if he understood.

Paul broke the silence. "Toss me a steak." The clatter of silverware against plates covered Caroline's rush of breath as she forced tears back. Curt's sweet spirit came to mind, and she suddenly felt like a traitor to him. Was it wrong to be here…enjoying dinner with Matt? She forced the thought from her mind. Matt was just being friendly. She would not ruin his gracious hospitality with her self-pity and guilty conscience.

Paul eased the awkward mood with a quick wit that complemented Andie's dry sense of humor. The two related stories about the horses they rode together, and Caroline soon found herself laughing.

"Stormy's a spitfire." Paul reached for a second yeast roll. "That horse doesn't like me at all."

"How did she get the name Stormy?" Buttery corn kernels spattered Callie's chin.

"She was very temperamental when she first came to live with me," Andie explained. "She was young, and she hadn't had the best of care."

Callie reached for a second ear of corn. "What does temp'mental mean?"

"Stormy's spirited. She has a lot of personality." Andy sipped from a glass of soda. "She's a bit stubborn, too, which a good thing if it's channeled right. Anyway, Stormy's my show horse now. I barrel race with her."

Callie cocked her head to the side and scrunched her nose. "What's barrel racing?"

"It's a kind of competition where horses race around barrels and try to beat a time without knocking any over." Andie slathered butter on her roll. "I'll show you when you come to the barn. Stormy likes barrel racing most."

"How do you know she likes it?" Callie's blue eyes shone bright with wonder. "Does she talk to you?"

"In a way, with body language." Andie tore a piece from the roll and slipped it into her mouth. "Most times you can tell what someone's thinking just by the way they look and how they act."

"Like I can tell when Mama's gettin' mad, 'cause her face gets a frown, and she crosses her arms real tight, like this." She demonstrated while Andie and Paul laughed.

"Wow, that's some look." Matt feigned fear. "I hope I never make your mom mad."

"Oh, you will," Callie assured him. "But she doesn't stay mad very long, unless you break her favorite picture frame 'cause you're runnin' in the house after she told you not to at least fifty-million times. Then she stays real mad, and it's no fun at all. No, sir!"

"I shouldn't have gotten angry over that." Caroline apologized. The photograph had been her favorite of Curt, the one she'd kept on her nightstand in the apartment. Callie had shattered it the week of his funeral. "It was just an accident."

"It's OK, Mama." Callie patted her hand. "I won't run in the house no more."

"Anymore."

"Right. Look what Paul made for me while we were outside." She flipped open her sketch book to a set of pictures. "He can draw all kinds of cartoons, and even princesses and castles. Aren't they beautiful?"

"They're very good." Caroline nodded. "Paul, you're quite an artist."

"Thanks."

"Oh, Mama, I know!" Callie bounced in her chair, shaking the table. Soda splashed over the rim of Matt's glass. "Paul can paint pictures on my bedroom walls!"

"Callie, that's a lot of work." Caroline dabbed the spill with her napkin, then placed a hand on Callie's shoulder to still her. "Paul has schoolwork and horseback riding lessons. I don't think he has the time."

"It wouldn't take me that long." Paul shrugged. "I've done murals at the high school. I did one of our mascot on the gym wall last month."

"See, Mama. He can do it."

Caroline looked to Matt, who nodded approval. "I think it's a great idea."

"Well…all right. That's very generous of you, Paul. We'll hash out the details later, OK?"

"Great. I can start next week."

"We'll clean up the kitchen, Matt," Andie offered as they finished eating. "I know how much Paul likes to wash dishes."

"Very funny." Paul groaned. "You wash. I'll dry and put stuff away."

"I'll wash!" Callie volunteered.

"We'll do it together," Andie settled things. She shooed Matt and Caroline toward the back porch. "You two go enjoy the moonlight."

"Well, if you insist." Matt slipped his hand into

Caroline's, and they walked into the crisp blue-black of night. She shivered at his touch and thought about pulling her hand back. It felt so odd, and yet something drew her to him. She twined her fingers with his, and stars winked as they walked a distance, then settled into a loveseat sheltered by a gigantic weeping willow tree. Its delicate leaves whispered in the breeze, and Caroline pulled her sweater tight with her free hand to ward off the chill.

"This tree must be very old. I've never seen one so tall."

"My grandfather used to joke he bought this weeping willow and got a ten acre bonus."

Caroline gazed over swells of pasture, barely visible in the dark. "Why was Paul so angry the night he fell into the Aronson's pond?"

"Oh, that." Matt sighed, leaned back in the seat, and stretched his legs. "He'd just come to live with me. He was having a little difficulty...adjusting to new boundaries."

"He looks just like you."

"He's my sister's son."

"What happened to her?"

Matt sighed. "I don't know. A lot of things. She's always liked to imbibe, even when we were younger, and that led to trouble. The last few years have been a struggle. She's detoxing at a rehab center in Nashville."

"What about Paul's father?"

Matt shrugged. "We haven't heard from him in years. He took off when Paul was eight and never looked back. It wasn't a bad thing, him leaving. He used to...abuse my sister."

"A tough road."

"It has been. Paul's had a lot to deal with, but it's

getting better every day, thank God. In the beginning, I thought I'd lose my faith. It wasn't just the difficulties with Paul. There were other factors, as well. I was skating on thin ice. But through it all, my faith's grown stronger."

"I wish I could say the same." Caroline's voice was thick with regret. "I must admit, I've wondered more than once over the past week what in the world I was thinking to quit my old job, uproot Callie from everything familiar, and come here. I just need..."

"We all need." Matt's voice reassured her. "It's OK to need, Caroline."

She leaned back in the swing and sighed. "There were just too many memories."

"Memories are like chocolate. Too much indulgence will make you sick."

"I know. It's just...hard. Most memories are comforting, and this..." She swept her hand across the unseen. "It's...a little scary."

"So is jumping off the high dive. But once you do it, you realize the anticipation was much worse than the jump itself, right?"

"Unless you belly flop." Caroline remembered a summer camp experience to that effect. "But I guess you're right, Matt."

He squeezed her hand. "So, you'll go to the church's potluck on Sunday?"

She smiled wistfully. "I guess so. What can it hurt?"

6

"Mama, come down here, quick!" Callie's sneakers slapped the wood floor as she ran to the foot of the stairs. "A lady's on the porch. She's gonna ring the doorbell."

As if on cue, the doorbell chimed. "Who is it, honey?"

"I don't know. She's a stranger, and you said to never open the door for a stranger."

"I'm coming." Caroline turned from a beautiful view of the pasture beyond Callie's playroom window and tried to force thoughts of Matt from her head. She'd gotten caught up in the moonlight and laughter last night, and had agreed to go to the church's potluck lunch tomorrow. *Why did I agree to such a thing? Now I'll have to undo it.*

She hurried down the stairs and peeked through the front window. "Who on earth...?"

A woman with wind-tossed blonde hair and cornflower-blue eyes smiled at her. She was dressed in faded jeans and a flannel shirt, and she held a pie pan wrapped in aluminum foil that reflected the bright morning sunshine.

Caroline eased open the front door. "Hello. May I help you?"

"Caroline Lafollette?"

"Yes."

"Hi." She jostled the pie into one hand and offered Caroline the other. "I'm Sue Aronson. You met my daughter, Andie, at Matt Carlson's house last night."

"Oh, yes." The door swung all the way open. "Please, come in."

"Thank you." Sue stepped into the house as Caroline held the screen door for her. "I brought you an apple pie. I hope you like apples."

"Oh, we love apple pie. Thank you so much!" She took the pan from Sue, and it was heavy with the weight of an ample portion of the fruit. Callie hopped, hoping for a better sniff of the sweet aroma, while Socks flopped on the floor at their feet and stretched lazily in sunlight that streamed through the doorway. "This is my daughter, Callie."

Sue bent to Callie's level and smiled. "Well, hello. It's nice to meet you. Andie told me so many wonderful things about you."

"Did you bring Stormy?" Callie asked. "I really want to meet her."

"No. I walked over this morning. It's warm with the hint of spring, so sunny and mild. I didn't want to miss out. Stormy is back at the barn waiting for Andie to take her for a ride. Andie said she might teach you how to ride horses, too."

"Maybe. Mama said we'll see, and that usually means yes, except this time it might mean a big fat no. Mama doesn't like horses much."

Sue laughed. "Well, Andie's an excellent rider, and very careful, so you'd be learning from the best."

"Would you like a cup of coffee?" Caroline offered. "I just brewed a pot of French vanilla."

"I'd love a cup, if it's no trouble."

"None at all." She turned toward the doorway.

"Come into the kitchen."

"Mama, can I go outside and play?" Callie scooped Socks from the polished wood floor. The scent of lemon-wax lingered.

"Yes, honey. Just stay close to the house, OK? Don't go near the pond."

"Yes, Mama."

Caroline led Sue into the kitchen where the windows were open and a gentle breeze whispered around them.

"You've worked wonders in here." Sue gazed at the gleaming linoleum and drank in cabinet doors that Caroline had scrubbed until they shined. "I can hardly believe it's the same kitchen."

"You've been here before?"

"Oh...yes. I checked in on Nora religiously...before..." She ran a hand over the countertop, as if remembering another time. "I'm so sorry, Caroline."

"Thank you." Caroline nodded curtly. She poured two cups of coffee and handed one to Sue. "Cream or sugar?"

"Black is fine." Sue sipped. "Mmm, it's good. I love French vanilla."

"Me, too." They settled at the table, and Caroline doled out slices of pie. "This looks delicious. I love cinnamon, especially paired with apples."

"It's my mom's recipe. She always doubles the cinnamon." Sue took a tentative nibble. "You're going to be working at the high school as a counselor?"

"Yes. I start Monday. How did you know?"

"You must have mentioned it at Matt's last night. Andie told me when she got home. I teach algebra there, and I remember how nervous I was, starting in a new place. I thought I'd come over and introduce myself, break the ice, so to speak."

"I'm so glad you did." Caroline sipped her coffee. The knot of tension that took her breath every time she thought about going into the high school on Monday morning, knowing no one, began to ease. "Tell me about the school. Do you like teaching there?"

"Eight hours a day with rambunctious, hormonal teenagers—what's not to love?" She filled Caroline in on the most important procedures and behind-the-scenes school information as she nibbled apple pie and sipped warm coffee. "Seriously, though, I've taught there fifteen years, and I don't know where all the time has gone. It feels like just yesterday that I first walked into my classroom with nothing but a stomach full of butterflies and a dream."

"So, you must have started when Andie was just a baby."

"That's right, along with her brother, Kyle. They're twins. They were born premature, so I had to take an extended maternity leave my first year of teaching. I thought I'd never make it back to the classroom. But here I am, still going strong."

"I hope I'll follow. It's been kind of...weird, settling in. Not in a bad way, just different from the city. I can see the stars here at night, and listen to the song of birds in the morning. No traffic, no smog. No..."

...wallowing in self-pity over losing Curt.

"I'd like to have you over, let you meet the horses. My husband and I board half-a-dozen, and keep two of our own. Andie would be glad to take Callie for a ride, teach her a little about caring for the horses. It would give her something to do, until she settles in at school."

"I don't know..." Caroline bit her lip, the coffee suddenly acid in her throat.

"Andie mentioned you had a bad experience with a horse when you were younger."

Caroline nodded. "I got thrown when I was six, on a pony ride at the county fair, of all places. Broke my arm, do not pass go, head directly to the hospital in an ambulance, sporting a concussion and a compound fracture. I haven't been on a horse since."

Sue steepled her fingers beneath her chin. "It's your call. Maybe if you come see the horses you'll feel better about it. Brown Bear is just that—a big old teddy bear of a horse. He's very gentle, loves kids."

"Well...Andie does seem exceptionally responsible, and Matt says he's known her since she was born."

"Yes. Matt and I go way back. We went to school together." She grinned. "In kindergarten, he used to chase me around the playground and throw worms in my hair."

"No!" Caroline laughed. "How awful!"

"Yeah, well, he was a little tornado of mischief back then. If there'd been a kindergarten reform school, he'd have been first in line. As it was, he kept the time-out chair warm."

"He's been very kind to Callie and me since we came here. We arrived in a terrible storm the first night and ended up locking the keys in the car. I thought Matt was an intruder, too, when I saw him in the house. *And* the car ran out of gas."

"Yes, Kevin mentioned he helped you. It's kind of like fate, isn't it?"

"More like user error."

"I don't know, Caroline. There may be more to it

than that." Sue speared a bite of pie, then continued softly. "Matt's a good guy. He's done a tremendous job with Paul the past several months. And let me tell you, it hasn't been an easy ride by any stretch of the imagination. He's had a rough time since he lost his wife."

Caroline's breath hitched. The words were a gut-punch. "L-lost his wife?"

"Yes. Two years ago." She paused, studied Caroline's expression. "Oh, boy. He hasn't told you yet, has he?"

"No." Her mind reeled.

"Oh, Caroline, I'm so sorry. Me and my big mouth...."

Caroline stiffened in her chair. Her mind raced with a million questions. "What happened to his wife?"

Sue pushed back from the table, and chair legs scraped the linoleum. "I shouldn't say anymore. It's not my place. I only mentioned it because I thought..." Her fork clinked against the dessert plate as she stood and carried the plate to the sink. "You'll have to ask Matt. It's for him to tell."

Caroline followed her to the doorway.

"Please forgive my forwardness. I'd really better be going now." She rushed through the living room. "Thank you for sharing the pie."

Caroline propped the screen door for her. "You're welcome. I'm so...glad you stopped by. It will be so much easier going to school Monday, knowing I'll see a familiar face."

"Yes. I'll look for you. And you can find me in room two-sixteen if you need anything. It's near the library on the second floor, not too far from your office." She stepped onto the porch and started down the stairs before turning back to Caroline. "Oh, I almost forgot to ask you something."

"What is it?"

"Matt said you have a beautiful singing voice, and I wondered if you'd come practice with the church choir for the Easter service. I know Easter's still six weeks away, but we like to get in plenty of practice. We *need* plenty of practice. And we really need good, strong voices like yours."

"Matt said I have..." She shook her head. "I don't know." Caroline felt torn as she watched sunlight glint off Sue's sassy blonde hair. She'd been so kind to come and ease worries about school. It would be wrong to deny this simple request.

"Please, Caroline. I'd be forever grateful to you." Sue's gaze was filled with such sincerity, Caroline couldn't possibly refuse.

"OK. I'd be glad to help out."

"Oh, thank you! Rehearsals begin this Wednesday after the evening meal. I'll swing by here for you and Callie. We can ride together."

"OK." There was no backing out now. She'd committed, however difficult and uncomfortable it might be. "And thank you again for stopping by, and for the pie. It was so kind of you."

"You're welcome, Caroline."

She watched as Sue cut a path through the pasture and around the pond, back over the hill toward her house, kitty-corner to Matt's.

He was married...had a wife. Why hasn't he shared that with me?

She felt an odd tug of hurt that she'd bared her soul to him about Curt, yet he'd held back sharing with her. But then she remembered the deep blue of his eyes, and knew whatever happened must have been painful, nearly unbearable. Maybe he just wasn't ready to talk about it.

∽∾

"Where're we headed so early on a Saturday morning?" Paul yawned hugely. "I thought I was gonna get to sleep in today."

"You did. It's after nine already. And we're going to Mrs. Winslow's house. I promised her I'd stop by this morning to repair the leak in her roof.

"Great." His flat tone said it was anything but. "She's the old lady who likes to pinch my cheeks and tell me how much I look like you."

Matt laughed. "That's right."

"Don't you know it's like child abuse to subject me to that?"

"Mrs. Winslow's been pinching cheeks for over fifty years. I survived it, and so will you."

"It's just not right." Paul pressed his palms to his face, anticipating the next painful pinch. "And her house smells funny, like stinky old mothballs."

"So, don't go inside."

"But she'll offer us something to eat, and of course you won't want to be rude. So we'll end up trekking inside after all. Then she'll spend the next hour talking about her granddaughters in California, and her five million great grandkids. It's worse than the genealogy in the Bible."

"An hour won't kill you."

"That's what you think. I don't know why you even bother doing jobs like this, where you get paid with tuna sandwiches and bitter lemonade. You make a ton of money doing the big stuff with your company."

"That's why I can afford to do jobs like this for people like Mrs. Winslow. It's not all about money, Paul."

Matt slowed the truck as they neared a modest one-story rancher that was sorely past its prime. Paul helped unload an extension ladder and carried roofing materials to the front lawn before reluctantly stepping onto the porch to knock.

Mrs. Winslow struggled with the door. "Oh, hello, young man." She was stooped over, with snowy-white hair so thin and wispy that patches of mottled scalp peeked through. "My, have you grown since I last saw you!" Her hand wavered as she grabbed a hunk of his cheek between her arthritic fingers and squeezed. Paul's eyes watered. "I declare, you look more like your handsome uncle every day."

Paul sucked in a breath as Matt looked on, not even attempting to hide his amusement.

"It's good to see you, Mrs. Winslow." Matt hoisted a tool pouch over one shoulder. "We'll need to get right to work because we have another job to do this afternoon."

"Oh, I see." She wrung her hands. "I'll pour you a nice glass of lemonade in case you get thirsty. Sun's beating down awful hard this morning. Spring's about on us, I guess."

"Yes, it is." Matt whistled as he positioned the ladder against the house. The screen door slapped as Mrs. Winslow went to fetch the tea.

"I can't believe you lied to her." Paul followed him up the ladder like a puppy at his heels, a tub of roofing tar in one hand. "We don't have another job today."

"Yes, we do."

"We do? Where?"

"You'll see. Now, hand me the hammer, and let's get this done."

When the roof was fixed, they stayed behind long enough to devour tuna sandwiches washed down by tangy lemonade while Mrs. Winslow shared an update on her grandkids, followed by a parting pinch to Paul's bruised cheek.

"Where now?" Paul rubbed the injured flesh, grimacing.

"I thought since we had roofing materials we'd head over and repair the shingles that were ripped from Caroline's roof during the storm last week."

"Didn't she say she was planning to go into town this afternoon to buy groceries?"

"Yes. I wanted to make the repairs while she's away."

"Why would you want to do that? Don't you want to see her?"

"I don't want to do anything that might make her feel uncomfortable."

"Oh. And you think she'll feel less uncomfortable when she comes home to find we've been up on her roof?"

"I guess we'll just have to take our chances. Caroline doesn't accept help easily. I think she's used to doing things on her own."

Paul shook his head. "Whatever."

On the short ride to Caroline's, Paul tuned into his favorite music station on the truck's stereo. Matt conceded; he was learning to choose his battles. And Paul was a big help with the roofing projects, so it was a small compromise, all things considered. He grinned as Paul rolled the window down and let the wind rush through his hair, drumming his hands on the dash in time to the beat of the music.

The crunch of gravel battled the music as he swung the truck into Caroline's drive. Her car was gone, as Matt had hoped. He switched off the ignition, against Paul's protests, and the sweet sound of silence filled the cab.

Once again, Matt and Paul hauled the roofing material and ladder from the truck.

"Were you paying attention when we fixed Mrs. Winslow's roof?" Matt slung the tool belt complete with a hammer and roofing nails over one shoulder.

"Yeah, I guess." Paul toted a pail of roofing cement. "Why?"

"You're going to do the work this time." Matt positioned the ladder against the house, motioned Paul up, and followed him onto the roof. "I'll walk you through it; then next time you'll know what to do on your own. You never know when you might need to make a repair like this."

"OK." Paul found his footing and scooted carefully to the damaged area. Matt knew he had a fear of heights, but the kid hid it pretty well.

They made a good team, working side by side. Patiently, Matt demonstrated how to seal any fractures in the tarpaper with roofing cement. Then he showed Paul how to nail down the shingles so they'd stay in place even in the most severe thunderstorm. Paul was a good listener and caught on fast. When they were finished, Paul slid down the ladder and loped across the yard to survey his handiwork.

"Cool." His eyes glimmered with pride. "The roof doesn't look like it's got a nasty case of the chicken pox anymore."

"You fixed that," Matt slapped him on the back. "Good job."

"Thanks." Paul hauled what was left of the roofing cement and their tools back to the truck while Matt carried the ladder and a bucket of nails.

"Hungry?" Matt asked, checking his watch. "It's nearly dinnertime. We've made a day of it."

"Starved. Let's head to the pizza parlor. Andie's working there today."

"Oh? When did she start?"

"Last week. She's saving money so she can drive. Her parents said she can borrow one of their cars when she turns sixteen in May if she pays her part of the insurance."

"Hmm...not a bad idea."

"Figured you'd jump on the wagon with them. That's why I'm a step ahead, applying for a job at the grocery store."

"Speaking of driving," Matt slid the ladder into the truck bed, then tossed the bucket in beside it. "I've been doing some thinking."

"Great." Paul winced, adding the cement and tool belt. "Hit me with it."

"Well, I thought we might find you a good used car, something reliable yet reasonably-priced. We can spend the next several months fixing it up together."

"Wow." Paul pumped a triumphant fist in the air. "You mean you'd really do that for me?"

"Yes, I would." Matt wagged a finger at him. "But the car would come with strict rules, and the first time you broke one, that would be the end of the car."

"Wow. Oh...just wow." Paul stumbled over his words. "I'll follow whatever rules you want. This is awesome! I can't believe you'd do it for me."

"You're an OK kid, Paul. Though you complain a bit, you do the work, even when I drag you out of bed on a Saturday morning and let Mrs. Winslow pinch the fire out of your cheeks. We'll start looking for a car next week." He tossed him the keys to the truck. "Guess we'd better start practicing. Since you have your permit now, you take the wheel. I'll ride shotgun."

༺❦༻

Caroline had the feeling something was different about the house when she pulled into the drive, but she didn't notice the blown shingles she'd gathered from the yard and stacked to the side of the front porch were missing until Callie pointed it out.

"Look at the roof, Mama! It doesn't have freckles anymore."

Caroline followed Callie's gaze and saw the roof had indeed been repaired. The bare spots that had been left when shingles were torn away by the storm were gone. The roof was intact.

"Who do you think fixed it, Mama?"

She considered the question only a moment before replying with utter certainty. "Matt."

"He's like a guardian angel, isn't he, Mama?"

Caroline smiled at the thought. "Yes, honey, I think he is."

She remembered what Sue had said that morning. Again, the thought of Matt being married at one time gnawed at her, and she felt a bit detached. A secret stood between them, something it was impossible for her to move past. She hoped he'd tell her about it on his own, and soon. And if he didn't, well...she'd cross that bridge when she came to it.

❧

"Ready?" Matt switched off the ignition and turned to Caroline.

"I'm not sure." She fidgeted with the seatbelt and gazed up at the pretty whitewashed church. Its steeple pierced the cloudless sky. "I don't think I can go inside."

"Do you want me to take Callie on ahead," Paul offered. "Andie's waiting for me in the children's wing. We could give Callie a tour."

"Oh, can I, Mama?" She kicked the seat with patent leather shoes. "There's a playground, Mama. Look?"

"We have a library, too, munchkin." Paul tapped her nose. "I know how much you like books."

"Oh, Mama!" She unlatched her seatbelt.

"You can go if you stay with Paul. Don't wander off." Caroline turned to kiss her. "I'll be right in."

"OK, Mama." Callie pushed open the passenger door as Paul came around. She grabbed his hand and skipped alongside him up the steps and through double doors into the church. The child's eagerness caused Caroline a pang of guilt. She'd been selfish to keep Callie away from church for so long.

"We can just sit out here," Matt offered. "We don't have to go inside."

Caroline shook her head. "Oh, that would be a barrel of fun, for sure."

He swept a strand of hair from her face. "I don't mind. I like talking with you. We could take a walk."

"As tempting as that sounds…" She surveyed the

crowded parking lot and the playground full of squealing kids. "I'll be OK." She wouldn't ruin his afternoon. "Besides, I promised Sue I'd sing in the choir, so I guess I need to do this…get it over with."

"You won't be sorry." He came around the truck and opened the door for her. "I can smell Mrs. Winslow's cherry cobbler from here, and Mr. Harrison's barbecued ribs."

Caroline laughed, despite the wasps swarming her belly. "You have a nose like a bloodhound."

"And an appetite to match." He quickened his pace. "Let's get inside before the food's all gone."

Caroline followed him toward the doors and her heart began to race. She felt lightheaded, and wondered if she'd make it up the stairs.

She paused. "Matt, maybe—"

The double doors opened, and Sue smiled at her.

"Hi, Caroline. It's so good to see you again!"

Her smile eased Caroline's fear. Maybe she could do this. Maybe it wasn't so bad, after all.

"What do you have there?" She took the platter from Caroline.

"Nothing fancy…just some chocolate chip cookies."

Sue lifted the foil and sniffed. "They smell delicious." She glanced at Matt. "Kevin's already been through the line. He saved you a piece of cherry cobbler."

Caroline splayed a hand across her belly. The wasps still stung, but not so much. "I like cherry cobbler, too," she managed.

"Come on inside." Matt took her free hand. "I'll share mine with you."

7

"How's your week so far?" Sue strode into Caroline's office and plopped into a chair near the cluttered desk. She crossed her ankles and took a mint from the ceramic bowl on the file cabinet. "Still standing?"

"It's been hectic, but good." Caroline set down the file she was working on and leaned back in her chair. "I've met with most of the senior class and plan to work my way through the underclassmen over the next week. I should be able to get everyone in by next Friday, introduce myself, answer questions, connect names and faces."

"Thanks for seeing Andie this morning, by the way. She told me you spent quite a bit of time with her going over scholarship applications and showing her college-related websites."

"You're welcome. With her outstanding grades and the many community service projects she's volunteered with, she's well on her way. She shouldn't have too much trouble if she stays focused over the next year or so."

"Well, that's a loaded cannon with the teenage hormones raging. It's a daily battle, although Andie hasn't given me too much trouble—yet. Her brother, Kyle, now he's another story. Kevin and I should be completely gray by now."

Caroline grinned ruefully. "Don't borrow trouble, Sue. Andie seems like she has a good head on her shoulders."

"Just wait 'til Callie's nearly sixteen, on the brink of driving, with her head stuck on a particular boy, and we'll see how well you deal."

"Point taken. But Paul seems like a responsible kid. Matt keeps a pretty tight rein on him, and you do the same with Andie. Not much room to stray."

Sue's eyebrows disappeared beneath side-swept bangs that brushed across her forehead. "You'd be surprised the creative lengths they'll take to get around the rules. But I suppose I'm not telling you anything you don't already know, being a school counselor and all."

"No. But I guess it doesn't really hit home until you're dealing with your own kids."

"You've got that right." Sue reached for another peppermint. "I'll come by your place at five to pick you up for choir practice. It's casual, so dress in whatever's comfortable. We'll eat dinner together then have a short Bible study before practice begins. And the kids are going to have a pizza party. Andie's been planning games and activities for them, and I think Paul's going to help her. So you don't have to worry about Callie. Those two adore her."

"Should I bring a covered dish to share?"

"Not tonight. Myron and Betsy cook on Wednesday nights. You met them at the potluck Sunday, remember?"

"Sure." They were an older couple, retired and filled with the desire to serve. Myron was stout, and thick around the middle with an easy, ready laugh. Betsy was tall, thin, and spry for a woman of sixty-something, and she organized the church's monthly potluck luncheons with the efficiency of a drill sergeant. They made an unlikely couple, but seemed more than content with the fit. And they'd put Caroline at ease from the start last Sunday, when she'd walked into the small country church alongside Matt, carrying chocolate chip cookies made from scratch, her heart thudding out of her chest with memories of the last time she'd stepped inside a church. "Myron made me laugh with his jokes about fishing."

"That's Myron for you. And Betsy loved your pie. She asked for the recipe, didn't she?"

"Yes. I'll bring it for her tonight."

"Good idea. She won't stop hounding you until you do." Sue stood and headed for the door. "See you at five."

Caroline reached for a peppermint and tossed the candy into her mouth. Sue's words echoed through her head.

Andie will be doing the childcare, and Paul's going to help her...

It meant Matt would be at the church, too. A shiver of anticipation danced up Caroline's spine and her stomach tightened. The thought of being near Matt again unsettled her. Waves of desire wrapped in uneasiness filled her belly. How could her emotions be so hopelessly conflicted?

She sighed and closed the file she'd been working on. The heat of peppermint in her mouth swept through her sinuses and cleared her head. She left the office, careful to lock the door behind her, and started down the deserted hallway. The students had made quick work of scuttling from the building following the final dismissal bell, and the only sound was the swish of a mop over tile as a custodian polished the ninth-grade hall.

She enjoyed working at the high school. The faculty had embraced her with helpfulness, and Sue had made an effort to personally introduce her to many of the teachers. She was beginning to feel like one of the family, and word had already traveled down the grapevine that Jill Rothgeb was planning to stay home with her newborn baby. So there was a good chance Caroline's position would become permanent. She sure hoped so. Part-time salary barely made a dent in the bills, even without rent to pay.

Caroline left her car in the high school lot and walked across the street to the grammar school. Sunlight kissed her face as a warm breeze danced. The air teased with a hint of spring. She knew Callie would be waiting inside the school building with Mrs. Brabson. The librarian had taken Callie under her wing, and graciously offered for her to wait in the library after school until Caroline arrived. Callie loved the opportunity to delve through shelves and shelves of books, to drink in fanciful words as if they were an elixir.

"Hello, Mrs. Brabson," Caroline called as she entered the library. The room smelled of cinnamon mixed with cherries, warm and inviting.

"Diane," Mrs. Brabson corrected. She was merely a few years older than Caroline, and photos of teenaged daughters and a smiling husband graced her impossibly-organized desk. "How are you today, Caroline?"

"Wonderful. It's just gorgeous outside, warm and sunny. A person can't help but be cheerful on a day like this." She walked over to Callie, sprawled on a neon-green beanbag chair among a sea of picture books. "And how is my little munchkin this afternoon?" She dropped to her knees to see what Callie was reading.

"I'm good, Mama. Look at this picture of stone soup. It looks yummy. Can we make some for dinner?"

Caroline chuckled and ruffled Callie's hair. "Not tonight. We're going to church."

"Really, Mama?" Callie closed the book and clambered to her feet. "Are we really goin' to church again so soon?"

Caroline nodded. "Yes. Mrs. Aronson is going to pick us up at five o'clock. So we'd better hurry home and get you cleaned up. You look like you mopped up the dirt from the playground."

"Aw, Mama." Her cheeks were smudged, her ankles ringed with soil above the fold of white-turned-to-dirty-gray ankle socks. And the curls on her head fanned out like wild corkscrews around her cherubic face. "We had runnin' races today, and I won! I beat Billy Sands, and everyone said he was fastest of all before I came. So now I guess I'm the fastest."

"Wow, that's great!"

"Yeah." Callie skipped over to Mrs. Brabson's desk. "Can I check out this book for tonight? I wanna read more about stone soup."

Mrs. Brabson looked up from the computer where she was busy entering book codes into the system. "May I," she politely corrected.

"*May* I check out this book for tonight?" Callie repeated. "I promise I'll bring it back tomorrow."

"Certainly." Mrs. Brabson took the book and scanned its barcode into the computer, then handed it back to Callie. "You have a good time at church tonight."

"Oh, we will! Thank you, Mrs. Brabson. See you tomorrow."

"Goodnight, sweetheart."

⮞⮜

The setting sun was a scoop of orange sherbet in the sky as Sue dropped Caroline and Callie at the children's wing of the church.

"I'll park while you take Callie to the playroom, and then meet you in the fellowship hall for dinner."

"Sounds good. See you in a few minutes." Caroline took Callie's hand as they entered the church and they wound their way down the polished tile floor to the children's wing. Paul and Andie were leading a group of kids in a game of Simon Says as Mrs. Jenkins, the director of childcare, set plates of pizza and cups of juice along several round tables. Caroline's belly gurgled at the spicy aroma of pepperoni.

"Be good." Caroline kissed Callie. "I'll be back after choir practice."

"Have fun, Mama." Callie squeezed her hand and then let it go. She sprinted across the room to join the game. There'd been no period of adjustment for Callie. She'd taken to the church immediately.

Caroline, on the other hand, still struggled with mixed emotions. She loved the fellowship and felt a sense of peace, yet something inside her still felt unsettled, like a ship on storm-ridden seas.

She shook off the feeling and strode to the fellowship hall. The aroma of barbecued chicken made her mouth water. She took a plate from the serving line at the kitchen and found Sue already seated at the table with her husband, Kevin.

Caroline joined them. "I never got to properly thank you for getting the keys out of my car," she said to Kevin as she slipped into a chair. "So…thank you."

"You're welcome." He bit into a roll. "All in a day's work. It's just part of my job."

"That may be so, but thank you anyway."

"Ready to sing?" Sue scooped a forkful of potato salad.

"As ready as I'll ever be." Caroline reached for her napkin. "I hope you won't be disappointed."

"Never." Sue offered her the salt and pepper. "Matt said you sing like an angel."

"He did?"

"Yes." She glanced up, smiled. "And speaking of Matt…"

Caroline followed her gaze as Matt swaggered to the table, his hands full of food and drink. "Hello, Caroline."

She knew he'd be there, yet Caroline became tongue-tied at the sound of Matt's husky voice. She curled a stray strand of hair over one ear and dipped her head.

"H-hi." It seemed hardly fair for him to look so calm when just the sight of him, dressed in jeans and a short-sleeved black polo shirt, smelling of clean soap and aftershave, reduced her to a bundle of raw nerves.

"Is anyone sitting here?" He juggled a plate piled high with barbecued chicken and creamy potato salad as he motioned to the empty seat beside her. "Mind if I take a load off?"

"G-go right ahead." She drew a breath and forced herself to sound normal, relaxed. She found the task tremendously difficult, so she focused on her food. The potluck had come and gone without him saying a word about his marriage, and she wasn't sure what to make of the feeling in her belly—an unsettling tumult of caution and longing. His silence put her on edge, and raised questions she tried to tuck away. Maybe he wasn't ready to move on to something more than friendship...and maybe she wasn't, either. But the tremble of her fingers, the quickening of her pulse as he eased into the chair next to her, told her otherwise.

"Not hungry?" Matt asked as he set his drink on the table and watched her push green beans back and forth across her plate.

"Not much." Where had her appetite gone? She'd been ravenous just minutes ago.

"Hmm..." Matt couldn't speak, because he'd just stuffed his mouth full of potato salad. He seemed to have no trouble eating. No trouble at all.

"Caroline, would you like some coffee?" Sue offered. To Caroline's horror, she'd witnessed the entire exchange. Sue's empathetic smile clearly told the story—she'd heard the falter of Caroline's voice, noted her trembling hands.

"That sounds wonderful." Caroline pushed her chair back, glad for the escape. "Tell me where it is and I'll get it."

"Don't be silly. Kevin and I will go." Sue grabbed her husband's hand before he could shovel another forkful of chicken into his mouth. "Right, honey?"

"What?" His eyebrows drew together as he slathered butter on a second yeast roll. "Coffee's in the kitchen, same as always. You girls go. We men are eating."

Sue glared at him. "But I need your help, *honey*." Caroline heard a thud and the salt and pepper shakers wobbled as Sue kicked him under the table.

"Ouch. Oh." Kevin's fork clattered against his plate. He coughed, swallowed, and his gaze locked with Sue's as she nodded toward the kitchen. "Yeah, you need my help."

Matt laughed. "Still as smooth as a freight train leaping the tracks, you know that, Sue?" He shook his head at Kevin and reached for the pepper. "As long as you're going, *honey*, bring me a cup of coffee, too."

Before Kevin could respond, Sue took his hand and hauled him from his chair. "We'll be back…soon."

Caroline sighed and shoveled chicken across her plate. "Well, that was…"

"Interesting…amusing?" Matt turned his blue eyes on her. "You look very pretty tonight, Caroline, I like that blouse. It's all fluttery and feminine."

"Fluttery?" The only thing fluttering was her heart. She set the fork down, gave up on trying to cut the chicken. The tremble of her hands matched her racing pulse.

"Cat got your tongue?" He took a dinner roll from the basket in the center of the table, tore off a hunk, and slid it into his mouth.

"I-I'm just conserving my voice to sing." She lifted her chin. "I don't want to embarrass myself. First night jitters and all."

"That's right. Sue told me you're going to practice with the choir tonight." His gaze slid over her, questioning. "That's all that's got you jittery? You're like a firecracker with a short fuse tonight."

"I...what?"

He finished the roll with a second bite, wiped his mouth with his napkin. "You know, we really should put ourselves out of this misery."

"What misery?"

"The anticipation...me...you." He drew a sip of tea, and his gaze narrowed as he studied her over the rim of the glass. "It's got you on edge."

"Well, I..." She reared back, ready to strike with her words. How dare he insinuate—

He reached across the table, brushed a strand of caramel hair from her brow, and his gentle touch coaxed her defenses down a notch.

"You have beautiful hair, Caroline. A man could get lost in the miles and miles of silky waves."

She couldn't breathe. Her pulse stuttered as he tucked the strand of hair behind her ear and leaned in. His breath warmed her cheek as he continued.

"I want to take you out. Just the two of us. Friday night?"

"I..." The words stuck in her throat as heat blazed through her...a wildfire of emotions.

"Seven o'clock, Caroline. Andie will babysit Callie. I'll drive her over when I pick you up." His tone refused to take no for an answer. "Wear something...fluttery."

"I...yes." The overhead lights danced, and the room seemed to whirl. It was hard to draw a breath. Thankfully, Sue and Kevin returned at just that moment, juggling four foam cups of steaming coffee.

"Sugar?" Sue asked, throwing Matt a knowing look.

"I'll take a double hit," Matt answered, winking. "I like it sweet." He ripped open the packets Sue handed him, dumped the sugar, stirred, and drew a long sip, as if to emphasize. "You should go sing with the choir now, Caroline. Sing like an angel. I'll be waiting when you're done, and I'll drive you and Callie home."

"But, Sue—"

"I'm all for Matt taking you home, Caroline." Sue reached for her folder full of song sheets. "You're not the only one who's had prayers answered tonight."

8

"Bedtime is nine o'clock, firm." Caroline's gaze slid from Andie to Callie, offering her firmest mother look. "Don't let her talk you into staying up any later to read stories, or she'll be a bear in the morning."

"I won't be a bear, Mama."

"Oh, yes you will." Caroline shook a finger. "And you have to be up early because Paul's coming to paint pictures on your bedroom walls, remember?"

"Oh, yes! He's gonna do a princess first, right by my bed." She clapped her hands while jumping up and down. "It's gonna be so pretty!"

"Here's my cell number, in case you need me for any reason," Caroline called Andie's attention to the notepad on the counter where she'd jotted the number, along with a few other notes concerning Callie's bedtime routine.

"We'll be fine." Andie flashed a reassuring smile. "I won't let Callie out of my sight."

"I know. I trust you, Andie."

"We're gonna play, Mama," Callie chimed in. "And then we'll watch a movie. Andie's gonna make popcorn in the microwave, and it'll smell all buttery, just like the theater. Right, Andie?"

Andie nodded. "That's right."

"And Socks is gonna watch the movie, too, 'cause it's got a cat in it, and he likes to watch movies with cats. But he might not like the dogs." Her face scrunched with worry. "Uh, oh. I hope the dogs won't scare him."

"My dogs like our barn cats," Andie said. "They all get along just fine."

"What's a barn cat?"

As Andie began to explain, someone rapped on the front door. "Hello?"

"We're in the kitchen," Caroline called to Matt. She watched Callie follow Andie like a shadow out the back door and into the yard. The two were a good fit, and that eased the nervousness gnawing her belly. She hadn't left Callie with a sitter while she went on a date...well...ever. And this was a date, no denying it, no matter how many times she told herself she was just going to dinner. *With Matt.*

"Wow, you look..." The words faded to a low whistle.

The burn was immediate, and spread from the base of Caroline's neck to the top of her scalp. "Thank you," she managed. She'd taken extra care with her makeup and hair, which cascaded down her back in soft waves. "You clean up pretty well yourself."

The sight of him made her heart do a funny little two-step. The neat khakis were tailor-made to fit the strength of his long legs, and the button-down navy dress shirt brought out the blue of his eyes. And those eyes were easing over her like a warm wave at high-tide.

"These are for you." He handed her a colorful bouquet of wildflowers wrapped in white tissue paper and tied with a pale pink bow. "I hope you like them."

"Oh, Matt, they're lovely." She pressed her face to the blooms and inhaled the sweet scent of lilac and daisies. "Thank you."

"Can I help you find a vase?"

"In the corner cabinet, top shelf. If you can get it down for me, it'll save me having to haul out the kitchen stool."

"No problem." He opened the cabinet, brought out a fluted, crystal vase Aunt Nora had probably filled with countless bouquets of flowers through the years. "It looks great in here. I like your collection of wicker baskets over the cabinet tops, and the sepia-toned photographs." He leaned in for a better look at one of the photos. "Hey, is that my barn?"

She nodded. "And I took this one of the pond last week. I liked the reflection of the trees coming into full bloom."

"Wow, they're good." He glanced at the others that lined the walls, nodded appreciatively. "You've brought this place into the twenty-first century without compromising its original qualities and nostalgia."

"I like to tinker with design and decorating. It's nice to have a place to work with. At the apartment where I used to live, there wasn't much room for experimenting with different ideas. So I like this...living here."

Matt set the vase in the sink, ran water to fill it three-fourths of the way. "That's good, because I like you living here, too." He stepped back to let Caroline arrange the flowers.

"You fixed the loose shingles on my roof." She nestled a daisy between two lilacs and sighed with satisfaction.

"I take the fifth."

"Callie thinks you're our very own guardian angel." Caroline set the vase, wild with a waterfall of blooms, in the center of the kitchen table. Sunlight refracted off the crystal, bathing the room in a rainbow. "Thank you."

"You're very welcome."

She went to the back door as Callie's squeals echoed across the yard. "Honey, I'm going now."

Callie changed direction mid-stride and galloped toward the deck. "Hi, Matt."

"Hi, sweetie." His smile was instant, the pleasure genuine. "How's Socks today?"

"Good." Callie carried the cat like a baby tucked in her arms. "He's been playin' hide and seek with the birds."

"Sounds like mischief to me."

"Uh huh." Caroline knelt to wrap her arms around Callie. "Be good, OK? Obey Andie."

"I will, Mama."

"You'll be asleep when I get home, but I'll come up and kiss you, and I'll see you when you wake up in the morning."

"OK, Mama." She kissed Caroline's cheek, tucked Socks under one arm, and spun to race through the grass, squealing with delight as a cool breeze ruffled her curls.

"Ready?" Matt offered a hand and led Caroline across the yard toward the driveway where he'd parked the truck.

"Yes." Caroline drew a slight breath at his touch. "I...guess so."

"You sound...unsure." Matt's eyebrow curved and he gave her a lopsided grin. "Should I play taps?"

"What? No!" Caroline squeezed his hand. "I'm sorry. I guess I'm just...a little nervous."

"Do you expect something to go wrong?"

"No. It's just…"

"Callie?"

"No. I'm sure she'll be fine with Andie."

Matt paused and drew Caroline toward him. Turning her to face him, he smoothed hair from her brow with gentle hands. "What, then?" His voice was just as tender.

Caroline leveled him a look. "I'm scared to death, that's what. Go ahead, laugh if you want."

"Laugh? Why would I do that?" He took her hand, pressed it flat against the soft cotton shirt covering his chest. "Feel that?"

"Your heart?" *And muscles, taut beneath the fabric.*

"Exactly. Count off the beats. It must be racing at three-hundred ticks a minute."

"Yes, I feel…it." Caroline let her hand slip from his chest as the knot in her stomach eased a notch or two. "OK, maybe I'm not the only one who's nervous," she conceded. "So, what are we going to do about this?"

"Let's see…" He eased in and stroked her cheek with his knuckles. His breath teased her neck. "How about we both set our nerves aside and have a good time? Think you can manage that?"

"I'll…try." She offered her hand, and Matt gently drew her close. The moment seemed to dance and whisper around them as he leaned in to brush his lips briefly, softly, across her forehead where he'd smoothed her hair just moments before.

"There, sealed with a kiss." His voice was a murmur, husky with longing. "Caroline, you're like a precious treasure just waiting to be discovered."

His words brought a smile to her lips. She paused for a moment, dared not to breathe. Desire rushed over her like a wave, threatened to toss her off-balance as though she'd been caught in the undertow.

Matt reached behind her and she heard a low click as he released the truck's door latch. She drew one breath, two before turning from him to ease into the truck. Matt followed.

"So, how'd you like singing with the choir last Wednesday?" He slipped a key into the ignition and the engine purred, drowning out the thud of Caroline's heart. They shifted into drive and tooled toward the road as if he hadn't just kissed her, hadn't unsealed a tomb surrounding her heart that had been airless, emotionless since...

"I-I had a great time." Caroline fumbled with her seatbelt until she heard the telltale snap. "Sue's so easy to talk to. I feel like I've known her all my life. And she knows so much about everything from algebra to singing to horses. I think she's convinced me to let Andie teach Callie to ride."

"You might as well let her. It's better for Callie to learn from Andie than to hop on a mare herself and end up getting thrown. And you know she'd do that, eventually, with so many horses around. Besides, Sue's always said it's better to stay busy than to stay in trouble."

Caroline laughed. "Good advice. I guess you're right."

"Score one for me."

"And speaking of staying in trouble, did you really chase Sue around the playground and throw disgusting worms in her hair when you two were in kindergarten?"

He grinned. "She told you about that, huh?"

"Sure did."

"Guilty as charged. I dug up the biggest, fattest

earthworms from my dad's garden, carried them to school in my pockets."

"You did not!"

"Uh huh. On a dare from Tommy Jenkins. When I threw them at Sue, she squealed and tore off across the playground, bawling her eyes out. She went home and tattled to her folks, and her dad came over to have a talk with my dad. Whew, he was mad! That was not a fun evening in my house." He grimaced, reliving the pain of the punishment meted out. "Let's just say the worms stayed in the garden after that, and I knew better than to act on anymore dares from Tommy Jenkins."

"And Sue?"

"By the end of kindergarten we were thick as glue, and we've been good friends since. She and her husband, Kevin—"

"I met him Wednesday night."

"Yeah, while she was kicking him under the table." He laughed and shook his head. "They've been...like guardian angels."

"And Kevin's the one who loaned you the tools to unlock my car door."

"That's right. He and Sue have both helped me through some tough times, and they've been a godsend to Paul, as well." The laughter eased, replaced by an undertone of pain in his eyes.

"It hasn't been easy, has it?"

"No. But I wouldn't trade having Paul here. It scares me senseless to imagine him running the city streets at all hours, getting into who knows what kind of trouble..."

Caroline touched his hand. "It's more than Paul, isn't it?"

He drew a sharp breath and gave one quick nod.

"Want to share?"

"No...maybe." He shook his head. "Yes, but not yet."

"OK." She gulped back disappointment. Trusting came hard, and his reticence only made it more difficult. Yet she knew pushing him to share wasn't the answer.

"Trust me, Caroline," he murmured, as if he read her mind. She blinked hard, nodded once and squeezed his hand.

"I'm trying."

They turned into a parking lot on the waterfront. "Carabella's Italian restaurant?" She read the marquee, glinting beneath sunlight as late-afternoon eased into evening.

"My friends own it. I hope you don't mind, but I phoned ahead and asked them throw something together for us. We can walk down to the waterfront to eat."

"That sounds nice. It's going to be a beautiful night."

"Yes, it is."

Matt took her hand. "Come inside with me. I'd like you to meet them."

Caroline walked with Matt toward Carabella's, along the river kissed by dusk. The dress she wore, a lilac rayon blend in a delicate floral print, caressed her legs as a breeze whispered around them. Matt opened the door to the restaurant and the aroma of marinara sauce and freshly-baked garlic bread forced butterflies from her belly.

The building was filled with families and couples tucked away at linen-covered tables and bathed in flickering candlelight. Voices swirled and danced in a quiet, expectant hush while soft piano music soothed.

A tall, raven-haired beauty with large, almond eyes rushed toward them as they approached the reservation desk.

"Matt!"

"Hello, Geena."

"We've been expecting you." She returned his embrace, then redirected her gaze. "And this must be Caroline."

"Yes." Matt squeezed her hand. "Caroline, meet Geena Carabella, co-owner of Carabella's Italian Restaurant."

"I'm so pleased to meet you." Caroline was immediately put at ease by Geena's gracious smile. "Your restaurant is beautiful. And you have such a magnificent location, right on the river."

"Thank you. We hope you will enjoy the food as much as the scenery."

"Oh, I'm sure I will. It smells delicious."

"Where's Antonio?" Matt peeked around the reservation desk.

"Fussing in the kitchen." Geena waggled her fingers. "He's putting the finishing touches on your meal. He wants it to be more than perfect."

As if on cue, a man came around the corner and bustled toward the lobby, carrying a large wicker picnic basket in one of his beefy hands.

"Ah, Matt, my friend. It is so good to see you!" He spoke with a heavy Italian accent. Taller that his wife by a foot and built like a brick wall, he gave the impression of an earthquake with the energy of eight on the Richter scale. "How is life? And who is this beautiful young woman at your side?"

"Antonio, meet Caroline."

"Ah, Caroline. Your name matches your beauty."

"Thank you." Heat blossomed across her face. "You are too kind."

"No. I am brutally honest." Laughter rumbled from his belly. "It's a good quality to have, most times."

"This picnic basket is gorgeous." Caroline caressed the finely-woven white wicker.

"Yes, of course. But not as gorgeous as the food inside it, if I may say so myself." Antonio turned to Matt, beaming with pride. "I prepared a sampling of each of our specialties, all superb, just as you requested. And I also included a carafe of our finest cappuccino." He paused to whisper conspiratorially to Caroline. "It's good for conversation. So, enjoy, both of you. Stroll down to the waterfront and eat beneath the moonlight before the food gets cold and loses its flavor."

"Thank you, Antonio. It's been good to see you, too." Matt laughed as he took the basket in one hand and reached for Caroline's hand with his other. "Goodbye, Geena. Keep him in line, OK?"

"Ah, I try. But it is such an all-consuming task." She brushed a hand across her brow and sighed dramatically. "You have a good night."

"Yes, a wonderful night," Antonio added, winking. "A *bella sera.*"

Piano music faded as the foyer doors slipped closed behind them. Caroline sighed while a breeze kissed her face. The night was unseasonably warm. "They're both very kind."

"We've been friends since college. Antonio's always had a heart as big as he is." Moonlight beckoned as he and Caroline meandered down the greenway trail toward the water. "He and Geena are perfect for each other."

"I can see that." Caroline motioned to a patch of grass beside the water's edge. "What do you think of that spot?"

"Looks perfect."

Stars were just beginning to shimmer against a velvet expanse of sky. Matt set down the basket and opened it.

"What's in there?" Caroline peeked over his shoulder as he pulled out a white linen tablecloth. "The food smells too good to be true."

"Oh, it's the best Italian food you'll ever have."

"You've sampled it a lot?" Caroline took one end of the cloth, and together they spread it over the grass.

Matt nodded. "You could say that. I built their restaurant. And when a kitchen fire broke out and the restaurant burned to the ground a few years ago, I helped them rebuild it. Plenty of opportunities for meals together."

"Are you kidding me?" Caroline settled on one side of the cloth and smoothed her dress over her legs. "You built that beautiful glass-enclosed dining room, the grand entrance and wonderful lobby? Oh, Matt, you *are* an amazing and talented builder."

"I don't know if I'd go that far." Something flickered behind the blue of his eyes as he joined her on the cloth, something defensive. "It's just...brick and mortar."

"It's so much more than that. It's history...and character." Caroline reached into the basket and retrieved containers of food. She spread them over the cloth like a gourmet buffet line. "It's a part of you."

"You mean that?" His hand brushed hers when he reached into the basket to help her. "You really feel that way?"

"Well, yes. You had a vision, took something that wasn't there and created it, made it real. It's beautiful, amazing. And you brought joy to Geena and Antonio, as well." She slipped her sandals off and tucked her legs beneath her as she sighed. "I'll bet you do that for everyone you build for."

"No. Not everyone." He let the comment hang. His pained gaze locked on hers, then he deftly turned his attention back to the basket. "Fettuccini—good. Antonio makes the best fettuccini Alfredo I've ever tasted. And his vegetable ravioli is out of this world. You're going to love it."

Caroline took the containers from him. "You're sad."

"No." He shook his head. "Just...memories."

She found two bottles of sparkling water and handed him one. "Please share."

"I'd rather not, Caroline. Not tonight. Not like this." His eyes were tender, pleading, as he took the water from her. "The evening's just too perfect. But I promise...soon."

"Matt..." A hoard of questions gnawed at her. "I'm not trying to push, but I'd really like to know."

"I understand." He removed foil from the containers and found white china plates and silverware wrapped in linen napkins. "But it's a story for another day. Please be patient."

"OK." She'd set her questions aside for now. The river glimmered with starlight and leaves sang in the breeze. She agreed—the night was too beautiful to ruin with painful memories. "I'm hungry."

"Me, too." He unwrapped the largest of the containers and groaned with satisfaction at the hearty aroma of Asiago cheese melted over robust tomato sauce that bathed a generous portion of penne pasta. "This is some of Antonio's best work."

"Mmm..." Caroline found a container of garlic knots drizzled in butter and dusted with parmesan cheese. "Look at these."

Matt took one and popped it into his mouth. "Tell me about your job at the high school."

"I've had a smooth transition, thanks to Sue." Caroline filled her plate with a sampling of the food and settled back. "You know I'm a counselor, and that I enjoy working with teenagers."

Matt gave her a lopsided grin as he twirled a finger beside one ear. "Which makes you certifiable, by most accounts."

"Maybe so. But it's never boring, that's for sure." Caroline swirled her fork, gathering a few linguini. "And I really like what I do."

"That's important...loving what you do."

Caroline uncapped her bottle and sipped water. "You love building, don't you?"

"Um hmm." He was quiet for a moment, staring out over the water. His nod was ever so slight. "Yes. There's something about the smell of sawdust, the feel of lumber in my hands that gives me a charge. I don't know why. I guess I'm just built that way. Sorry for the pun."

Her gaze narrowed. "You fixed my front stairs, didn't you?"

He feigned innocence and reached for a slice of cheese-drizzled Panini. "I don't know. Did I?"

"All I know is they were rotted and falling apart

when I left for work yesterday morning, and when I got home in the afternoon they were solid and safe. And the broken shutters outside Callie's bedroom window were fixed, too. No more rattling against the windows in the middle of the night."

Matt shrugged. "Paul did that. I just gave him a little bit of guidance. I figure it's good for him to learn how to use a hammer and nails, a level and a ladder. And you mentioned the noise scared Callie and woke her during the night."

"I feel like I'm in the story, "The Elves and the Shoemaker.""

Matt grimaced. "I'm not sure I like being compared to an elf."

"If the shoe fits…" Caroline smirked. "Look, Matt, I appreciate all you've done, but you really have to stop."

"Why? You need the work done, and I enjoy doing it. And Paul's learning, too. That's a perfect combination, right?

"No. Not right."

"Why?"

"Because I don't know how I'll ever repay you."

"I haven't asked you to repay me, have I?"

"Not yet."

Matt's expression flashed from puzzled to wounded in an instant. He speared her with his gaze. "So, that's what you think this is all about?"

"I-I'm sorry." She set her plate down. "I've offended you."

"Yes, but I'll let it go because you don't know me very well, yet. If you did, you'd never even begin to think along those lines. I'm not that kind of man, Caroline."

She fumbled over words. "I didn't mean it that way. I just meant...well..."

He waited for her to finish.

"OK, I suppose I *did* mean it that way." She dabbed the corners of her mouth with her napkin, then twisted the cloth in her fingers. "But I didn't know..."

"Now you do."

He took the napkin from her and twined his fingers with hers. She felt gentleness, tenderness, in his calloused palms.

"You have to know you're safe with me, Caroline. I'm not using my carpentry skills to guilt you into doing anything you're not completely comfortable with. Don't get me wrong, I'm attracted to you."

She drew a breath, her heart quickening with his words.

"But I'm also a good friend, if that's all you're looking for. I'll still give your house a facelift brick by brick, because I like doing it. Besides, you've got a great kid and a cute cat, and you make a mean cup of coffee. What more could a guy ask for?"

"I don't know." She rocked to her knees, then stood and paced beneath the moonlight as stars watched overhead. "But good friends can talk to each other about...anything, right?"

"I suppose," he nodded. "when the timing is right."

"Then I'll wait, Matt, for your timing."

9

"Mama, they're here!" Gravel crunched beneath the truck's wheels as Matt came up the driveway. Callie put Socks down and ran across the grass. "Hi, Matt! Hi, Paul! Did you bring the paint?" She pressed her face against the window glass.

"Oh, no. I forgot." Paul plastered on his best disappointed look. But when Callie's smile wilted like a deflated balloon, he quickly gave in. "Just joking. It's in the truck bed, in a box. Hang on and I'll show you."

Callie backed away as Paul opened the passenger door and slid from the truck. He hoisted her into his arms so she could peer inside the truck bed.

"Yeah!" The smile returned as she clapped her hands in delight. "I colored the pictures you drew in my sketchbook, just like you asked, so you'll know which paint to use."

"Good job, munchkin." He set her down and patted her head. "Let me see them."

"They're on the kitchen counter. C'mon!" She grabbed his hand and dragged him along as if it was the most natural thing in the world to see a petite six-year-old haul a lanky teenager just this side of manhood alongside her.

Caroline watched from the porch, laughing.

"Hey, Caroline," Paul called breathlessly as Callie tugged him up the porch steps. "I'm here to paint the munchkin's room."

"It's all yours. Have fun."

His tennis shoes slapped the wood as he crossed the porch. He and Caroline had sat down together a few days ago to discuss the project like two businessmen cementing a high-powered deal. Caroline had shown him Callie's room, and they'd decided together which drawings would go where. Then he and Caroline had negotiated a wage for his work.

"Callie," Caroline braced her hands on her hips as she scooted in front of the door to block Callie's path. "You'd better stop pulling Paul's arm. He'll have a tough time painting left-handed."

Callie paused long enough to consider this. Then she dropped Paul's right arm, grabbed his left, and continued tugging as she sidestepped Caroline and scooted into the house.

Matt stood in the drive, watching. Caroline gazed at him, her belly knitting into a tight ball. Last night was wonderful...and unsettling. Questions still gnawed at her.

The ball loosened a bit when Matt shook his head and laughed. "Callie's a little firecracker. Comes by it honestly, I guess."

That took a moment to register. "Hey!" Caroline tried her best to look offended, but laughter punched through. "That's not funny."

"Is to me." He winked and then turned to unload supplies from the truck bed.

"Let me help you." Caroline's gaze swept over a circular saw, boxes of nails, pressure-treated lumber in varying sizes, sawhorses, and a humongous steel toolbox. "Wow. What's on the agenda today?"

"Back deck's rotting in a few places. I'd hate for

you or Callie to find a weak spot, maybe lean against the rail and fall. Thought I'd shore it up until we can rebuild the whole thing."

"I know a little bit about swinging a hammer," Caroline offered. "I can help if you'd like."

"Great." He hoisted the toolbox in one hand and the saw in another. "I'd enjoy the company."

She reached for a box of nails. "And then you'll stay for dinner?"

He nodded. "If you're cooking, I'm staying."

"I put a roast in the crock pot, along with some vegetables—no lima beans included."

"Dessert?"

"Of course." She followed him toward the deck. "Warm peach cobbler topped with homemade vanilla ice cream."

"Count me in."

"It's settled then." She opened the toolbox he set on the deck stairs and surveyed the assortment of tools before reaching for a hammer. "Where do we start?"

"Give me a minute." He took the hammer from her. "You change out of that pretty sundress and into something that can get messy while I grab the lumber from the truck. Then we'll take a look, decide together."

‎‎‎‎‎‎‎‎‎‎‎‎‎‎‎‎‎‎‎‎‎‎‎‎‎‎‎‎‎‎‎‎‎‎ঌ৵

Matt was impressed by the way Caroline swung a hammer. Her accuracy was amazing for someone who wasn't used to working with tools. No smashed thumbs or bruised fingers...yet. He grinned as she brushed stray hair from her brow and bit her lip, deep in concentration. Her hair, falling from the loose ponytail she'd gathered it into, shined like a newly-minted coin in the early-spring sunlight.

Guilt gnawed at him. He'd stubbed up last night when she started asking questions about Mandy, and that was wrong. She had a right to ask...and to get some straight answers. It wasn't fair to ask her to trust him when he couldn't come clean about something so important.

"Hot for March, isn't it?" He said, even though he was used to working in the heat and enjoyed the feel of the sun warming his back through a white cotton T-shirt. But her face was flushed, her brow damp. "Let's take a break."

"I'm fine." She aimed the hammer, took another swing at a nail that sunk neatly into the two-by-six he'd set. The sound echoed like gunfire off the house and across the pasture, startling birds from the weeping willows along the pond. "We don't have much left to do."

"It'll wait." Matt took the hammer from her. "Come sit in the shade, and I'll get you something cold to drink."

"OK." She swiped a stray hair from her brow. "Maybe just a quick rest. I made lemonade earlier."

"Sounds good."

He eased her beneath the shade of the porch awning, and then went through the screen door and into the house. The delicious aroma of simmering meat slathered in gravy made his mouth water. Music spilled from Callie's room, mingled with the sound of her laughter. Paul had brought his iPod dock, and he sang along with the songs.

Matt hunted for two glasses, found them on the low shelf to the right of the sink. Cool air spilled from the refrigerator when he opened the door. The shelves were stocked, a far cry from the day he'd brought sacks of food. The lemonade was fresh-squeezed and tangy, not from one of those clumpy, powdery mixes. He tossed plenty of ice into the glasses and poured.

He found Caroline sitting cross-legged against the house, gazing across the pasture toward the mountains.

"It's so peaceful here," she murmured as she took the glass he offered. "Sometimes I feel like I'm caught in a dream, it's so unreal."

"Still not missing the city?"

She gave a small snort. "Hardly. Like I said—traffic, smog, congestion, noise. What's there to miss?"

"I don't know...friends?"

"When Curt died, I lost my best friend, so there really wasn't much left to miss." She studied him over the rim of the glass, her honey eyes huge.

"I'm sorry, Caroline."

"I know." She nodded, then motioned toward the back of the house. "The deck looks good. You do good work."

"*We* do good work." He offered her one of the chocolate chip cookies he'd found on a platter she'd set out on the kitchen counter. "We make a great team, don't you think?"

"Yes, I guess we do." She nibbled the cookie, then drained the glass and rolled it between her palms. Condensation left a trail of moisture across her jeans-clad leg. "Matt, I think you have a tremendous gift for taking the worn out and broken and transforming it into something beautiful."

"That's...nice." The words surprised him and gave him courage. "Have you ever had such a deep passion for something that it threatened to consume you?"

"I'm not sure what you mean by that."

He shifted uncomfortably and eased his back flat against the house. "I'm sorry about last night, Caroline. You asked me a question, and I avoided the explanation. It was wrong, and I have something to tell you, something that needs to be said, but I don't know where to start."

"The beginning's a good place."

"I guess so." He chose his words carefully, his steady voice refusing to betray the fact that his heart had kicked into overdrive.

"When Mandy and I met, I was just starting my construction business. It was backbreaking work, both physically and mentally demanding, but I was determined to make a go of it, build something lasting and strong." He sipped lemonade to soothe the dryness from his throat. "I took on small jobs at first, anything to get my name out there and prove I was the real deal. My folks noticed I was good at fitting things together, taking a vision and making a run with it. They encouraged me to give college a go, to get a degree in business so I'd understand that side of it. So I did."

Caroline's eyes narrowed and he wondered what she was thinking. Would his explanation...this admission...push her away? He forced out the next words. "I met Mandy at a home show, where she was working a booth for a local landscaper. We hit it off, and married within six months."

He heard her slight intake of breath, noticed her grip on the lemonade glass tighten so her knuckles turned white, yet Caroline remained silent.

"I worked insanely long hours, and at first it was OK. Mandy had big dreams for us, and she liked nice things. But the jobs started getting bigger, and the hours grew even longer." He shook his head. Things had quickly gotten out of hand. Work was a wildfire raging out of control. "I should have been content with the early success and let the business level off, but I was restless. The more I built, the more it consumed me. I kept telling myself I'd slow down eventually, take Mandy for a long vacation, but the right time never seemed to come. She quickly tired of being left alone on the weekends, of waking in the morning to find me already gone. We argued more and more."

The memory shamed him.

"Then she told me she was pregnant."

His gaze followed Caroline as she stood and placed her glass on the deck railing, then turned her back to him and stared into the pasture beyond. "We'd discussed having kids, but were waiting for things to settle down. Even so, I was thrilled. The only thing I wanted more than success with the business was a child. I promised Mandy I'd cut back and refuse any big jobs for a while, and I meant it. Things got better at home. Mandy was happier than I'd seen her in a long time. She loved feeling the baby kick, drank in all the attention. We sat together at night going through baby name books, poring over the ones we liked best, deciding which would be perfect for our child."

He stood and went to Caroline. Tears shimmered and her lips quivered as she turned to face him.

"Then Antonio and Geena's restaurant burned, and they asked me to help them rebuild. They were my friends, and in a terrible spot. I'd built the restaurant for them, so I knew it like the back of my hand. I just couldn't turn them down. Mandy was livid when I told her. You see, the work was going to be intense, and the baby was due in less than two months. But I went ahead, signed on anyway. I didn't consider what Mandy needed, just kept right on doing my thing."

"Oh, Matt." Caroline pressed a fist to her mouth as her tears spilled over to run down flushed cheeks. "You don't have to…"

"Yes, I do." His shoulder brushed hers as he continued. "Then one night I stayed longer than I'd meant to. The inspector was coming by first thing in the morning, and we were having some problems. I didn't want to leave without putting things in order. I felt I owed Antonio and Geena that much. If we didn't pass inspection, it might mean weeks of lost business for them, and they were already experiencing serious financial struggles. So I stayed and did what needed to be done."

Caroline nodded. "You were loyal…to your friends."

"Yes, but not to my wife." The words, the admission, came with great difficulty. "Mandy was furious with me by the time I finally got home. She'd had mild contractions off and on throughout the day, and she was scared. And that fear led to anger. When I told her she should have called to let me know, she screamed that it wouldn't have done any good, since I was married to my work, not my wife. She was inconsolable, and she stormed out of the house, got in the car, and squealed off into the night."

The painful memory of what happened next choked him. "She hadn't gone two miles when she missed a red light and was hit by an oncoming SUV. It totaled the car, killed her instantly."

Caroline gasped. "But the baby…?"

Matt shook his head. "Our baby girl died that night, too."

Caroline stroked hair that cascaded across his forehead. "Oh, Matt, I'm so sorry. I can't imagine..."

"Such ugly words, such regret. It was my fault, all of it. I was so selfish."

"No." Caroline grasped his hand. "It was an accident."

"I should have been there for her."

"You were helping your friends."

"Yes, but—"

"No." Caroline pushed back from the rail to pace the length of the deck. "Sometimes things just happen. It's not always meant for us to understand why."

"You're not playing fair, Caroline." Matt drew her to him and brushed a thumb across her damp cheek. "You're supposed to flash a condemning look, murmur something shallow and condescending, then walk away."

"Sorry to disappoint."

He touched two fingers to her chin, leveled his gaze with hers, saw the compassion, the empathy, and knew she understood his pain in a way no one else ever could."

"Will you pray with me, Caroline. I feel...I need..."

"Of course."

Matt grasped her hands, and his voice soothed as it resonated over the music and laughter pouring from Callie's room. "Father, thank You for this beautiful night, for Your never ending grace and forgiveness. Be with us as Caroline and I get to know each other and begin to trust. Bless us with Your wisdom and guidance, Your will." He fell silent, squeezed Caroline's hand as he added his own private requests.

Lord, let me put Caroline's needs first, without

selfishness. Let me be mature and humble, not self-serving and foolish. Don't let me do anything to hurt her. Hold me close to you, Lord. Guide my steps.

10

"Place your foot in the stirrup like this." Andie demonstrated the mounting technique. Then she slid from Brown Bear and hoisted Callie into the saddle. She helped Callie hook her foot neatly into the stirrup. "Good job. You look like a real cowgirl now."

"It's high up here!" Callie gripped the saddle horn with one hand while she adjusted her riding helmet with the other and glanced toward Caroline, who stood at the riding ring's gate. "I can see our house, Mama."

"Yes, it's just across the pond." Caroline nodded and smiled to hide her nervousness. The horse was so big...and Callie so small. What if he bucked, or took off running and dumped Callie onto the ground?

The sun warmed her back through her cotton T-shirt, and a breeze ruffled her ponytail as she watched Andie maneuver around the horse with confidence. It would be OK...Callie was having fun, and Andie was careful, just as Sue had promised she'd be. Caroline leaned against the gate and breathed in the scent of wild onions mixed with hay and damp earth. She savored the rich smell...so different from city smog.

"Let me show you what to do next." Andie guided Callie through the paces of holding the reins correctly, then guided Brown Bear through a few careful steps.

"I'm ridin', Mama." Callie bounced slightly in the

saddle as the horse stepped across the grass. "Look at me!"

"I see you, honey." Caroline fought the urge to pull Callie from the horse and gather her into safe arms. Instead, she waved as Callie smiled into the sunshine. "You're doing great."

"Wow, that's awesome." Paul came to stand beside her. He propped one boot-clad foot onto the fence rail and pulled a ball cap low across his forehead. "It took me weeks to get up the nerve to do even that much."

"Callie's got no fear." Caroline frowned a bit. "I'm not sure whether that's a good thing or a bad thing."

"Andie will keep her safe." He crossed his arms and slouched against the fence. "She only beats up on unsuspecting city boys who have a serious fear of horses."

"You've been thrown?"

"Not yet. But I've fallen off Brown Bear a few times, and I won't get near Stormy." He shrugged. "That horse has it in for me, but she loves Andie. They have a weird connection that I don't even try to understand." His gaze followed Andie as she led Brown Bear by the halter. "Andie's a natural around horses. She started riding when she was two, and barrel racing when she turned seven. Her mom used to barrel race, too. It must be in their blood."

"Maybe so." Brown Bear picked up the pace a bit, her gait relaxed and steady, and Callie's delighted squeals echoed across the pasture. "Do you really think Callie's safe?"

"Besides having a seriously sore rear end from the bouncing, yes. Andie will guard the little munchkin with her life. She's stubborn that way."

Caroline noted the look in Paul's eyes, deep blue as Matt's. "You like Andie, don't you?"

"You could say that." He shrugged, but the grin on his face denied nothing. "For a stubborn and opinionated girl, I guess she's OK. We'll see what happens."

"Sounds pretty serious to me." Caroline laughed. "You have it bad."

"Maybe...yeah."

The deep blush that splotched his face, the way he shifted feet and tugged the ball cap lower to hide his eyes, told Caroline she'd better change the subject—fast. "How are the murals coming?"

"I just finished. I think they look pretty good."

"I'll bet they do. I'll let Andie know we're going to the house for a quick look. She'll walk Callie back when they're finished."

Satisfied that Andie had things under control with Callie, Caroline followed Paul around the pond to the house and up the stairs to Callie's room. Sunlight flooded the window to illuminate vibrant colors in the murals splashed across each wall. A mermaid was spectacular in her glittery, sparkling fish tail, and animated mice, dressed in topcoats and ball gowns, held hands as they appeared to leap from the wall over Callie's bed.

"Oh, the ceiling..." Caroline's breath caught as she gazed up at the galaxy of stars Paul had painstakingly feathered with glow-in-the-dark paint.

"You like them?"

"They're incredible...amazing."

"They'll illuminate the room at night, so the munchkin won't be afraid of the dark."

"That's so thoughtful." Caroline patted him on the

back. "Oh, Paul, you've done a wonderful job."

"Thanks." The crimson kiss of blush deepened. "It's nothing."

"Nonsense." Caroline turned toward the door. "We need to celebrate."

He followed her. "Chocolate chip cookies and soda?"

"For starters. Come down to the kitchen. I'll check on Callie, then toss together a fresh batch of cookies while you pour the drinks."

"I'm in." He rushed through the doorway, and Caroline heard the slap of his tennis shoes against the stairs.

She went out to the porch and saw Callie and Andie still working together in the riding ring. Callie's delighted squeals resonated across the pasture as she circled the fence. Caroline backpedaled to the kitchen, where she mixed flour, sugar, eggs, vanilla, butter, and a mountain of chocolate chips as Paul filled glasses with ice and poured soda.

"You make these a lot?" Paul leaned against the counter and watched, fascinated, as she blended everything together with a wooden spoon.

"Uh huh. They're Callie's favorite."

"The munchkin's got good taste." He snatched a bit of batter from the bowl and popped it into his mouth. "Mmm...my mom never made cookies like these."

"Maybe she was busy working. It's not easy for a single mom to do it all, you know."

"Nah." He shook his head and washed down the nibble of batter with a swig of soda. "She was flat on her back, passed out from the drinking. She couldn't keep a job. We moved a lot, changed schools a lot. It su—I mean, stunk."

Caroline glanced up. "That must have been rough. I'm sorry."

"Don't be. I like it here. First time I've stayed at the same school for more than three months straight." He lifted the ball cap, ran a hand through matted hair, then tugged the cap back on again as he slouched against the counter. "Uncle Matt's tough, but he's all right. He's going to help me get a car, you know. We've been looking together. I'll have to work for the gas and insurance, though. He says I'll appreciate it more if I put something into it, too."

"Sounds reasonable."

"Yeah." He polished off the soda and refilled his glass. "I'll be working some nights and Saturdays down at Bartlett's Grocery, bagging. It doesn't pay much, but at least it's a start."

"When will you be sixteen?"

"Three months, twelve days and—" He checked his watch. "Nine hours."

Caroline laughed and spooned the dough onto a baking sheet. "How much do you know about fixing things around the house?"

He shrugged. "Uncle Matt takes me with him a lot when he does construction jobs. He shows me how to do stuff."

"Yes. He told me you repaired the shingles on my roof, and fixed the broken shutter outside Callie's bedroom window."

"He did?" Caroline thought he stood just a bit taller. The grin on his face was contagious.

"Sure. So I thought we might discuss some business while the cookies bake. You did such a great job on Callie's room; I've got a list of things I'd like you to work on around here."

"Cool. When can I start?"

࿇

Matt followed his friend, Jim Harrigan, across his backyard as they surveyed the rear of Jim's house. He'd phoned Matt the week before, asking for help with a 'Top Secret Project' for his wife in honor of an upcoming wedding anniversary.

"I've got a pretty good idea of what you want, but let's go over things once more." Matt flipped open a sketchpad and checked his notes. "I need every detail, every nuance you're looking for."

Jim nodded, and motioned to a small back window tucked along the siding of the house. "Let's start here."

"It's as good a place as any." Matt scribbled while Jim rattled off details.

"Janie leaves for her mother's in Sacramento on the first flight out in the morning, and she's only planning to be gone ten days." Jim Harrigan glanced at his watch. His graying hair glinted in the sun. "Do you really think you can get all the work done in time?"

Matt smiled at the man he thought of as a father. "Sure. With your help and my nephew's, it shouldn't be too difficult. Let's just pray for good weather."

"I'm a step ahead of you on that. I hope it's worth the agony Janie's put me through these past weeks. She thinks I don't want to go with her to visit her mother because I'm planning to spend the week golfing and carousing with my buddies."

"Well, won't she be surprised when she sees what you've done in honor of your thirtieth wedding anniversary?"

"Can't wait for that. She's always wanted a solarium filled with plants, a place to relax and read those romance books she loves so much. With the last kid grown and off to college, she'll have plenty of time for that."

"And you'll have plenty of time to golf."

"That's the plan." He slapped Matt on the back, and then hiked up his waistband around a spreading paunch. "What's next?"

"I'll head to the building supply store when I leave here and place the materials order." Matt scribbled a final note on the pad and flipped it closed, then tucked it into the back pocket of his jeans. "Everything seems to be in order. I'll be back first thing in the morning to get started. You'll know by the roar of my circular saw ripping through the dawn."

"You sure do earn your keep."

"I make it my business to do good business."

"Tomorrow, then?" Jim slapped him on the back.

"Tomorrow." With a parting nod, Matt climbed into his truck and started home. Building the solarium would demand a good chunk of his time the next week or so, which would mean less time with Caroline. But he'd given his promise to Jim, and he intended to keep that promise. He just hoped history wasn't repeating itself.

❧❦

"Mama, do you think I did a good job riding today?" Callie asked as Caroline tucked her into bed.

"I think you did a fabulous job, sweetheart."

"Andie said if I work real hard, maybe I'll get

good enough to ride Stormy. I think Stormy likes me, Mama. She ate part of an apple out of my hand. Andie said she won't do that for Kyle or Paul, even."

"Just don't ever mount her without Andie's permission. It's very dangerous to do that. Understand?"

"Yes, Mama." She yawned hugely, eyes heavy with sleep as she gazed up at the stars Paul had painted. "I love my new room, Mama. The ceiling looks like Heaven."

Caroline stretched out on the bed beside her and lay there beneath the soft glow. "It *does* look like Heaven. Paul did a great job."

"He's nice, Mama. And Matt's nice, too. I'm glad they're our friends."

"Me, too." Caroline's breath caught as all the worries over moving, and whether or not Callie would adjust to the change, fled. "I'm glad you like it here."

Callie wiggled beneath the blankets and scratched her nose, then fixed her gaze on the glowing ceiling stars once more. "Do you think Daddy can see us?"

"I don't know, honey." Caroline's gaze swept the pasture beyond Callie's window and settled on a glow of lights coming from Matt's porch. "But if he can, I'm sure he's smiling."

❧❧

The front door slammed, rattling the papers Matt sifted through. Paul was home from dinner at the Aronson's house. Matt drew a breath anticipating the inevitable shout out.

"Uncle Matt?" Like clockwork, Paul hollered down the hallway. "You home?"

"In my office." Matt reached for an invoice. "I'm drowning in a sea of paperwork."

Footsteps pounded the polished wood floor. Paul strode through the doorway, took one look at the mess of papers, and shook his head. "I keep telling you to hire a secretary or an office manager to help you organize this mess. Better yet, just call a garbage truck to haul it all off."

"Very funny." Matt pushed aside a stack of papers, clearing a space on the desk for his coffee mug. His laptop's screensaver clicked on and a rainbow of fishes swam in perpetual circles beneath an electronic sea. "Sit down. We need to talk."

Paul slouched into an armchair. "Uh oh, what did I do?"

"More like what you didn't do."

"Take out the garbage? Wash the dishes?"

"No...and no."

Paul's knee began to bounce. He clasped his hands in his lap. "Then what's wrong? You look serious."

"I *am* serious." Matt hesitated only a moment. "I know you don't want to hear this, but your mother called."

"What, she lost her job already? Or maybe she's kicked out of rehab again?" Paul's eyes flashed, betraying the hurt he felt, the anger and distrust that plagued him.

"She wants you to call her back. I promised her you would."

"Well, you shouldn't have. I don't want to talk to her."

"You can't just ignore her, Paul. She's your mother, whether you like it or not."

"Well, I *don't* like it. So, *you* call her back."

Matt sighed, pinched the bridge of his nose to ward off the tension headache about to rip through his head. "I know she's hurt you, but she's trying to do better. We need to try a little, too."

"That's not fair, Uncle Matt." Paul stood stiff and stone-faced in the doorway. "Don't play that card. It stinks. This whole thing stinks. I hate it. I hate...*her*."

The force of his words wounded Matt, and he wondered if the two people he loved would ever heal from the hurt they'd been dealt. Eydie's life hadn't been easy. Sure, she'd made some bad choices, and the consequences were steep. But she wanted better, and without their encouragement she was doomed to continue the cycle. Paul was too young—and too hurt—to understand that. But Matt saw Paul's side, too, and understood his fear of having his heart broken yet again. Eydie hadn't exactly kept the promises she'd made in the past, and what promise did he have that this time, finally, the outcome might be different?

Matt felt as if he were being ripped in two. He leaned forward and placed a hand on Paul's knee.

"You're mad, and you're hurt. I don't blame you for that. You hate what she's done, but you don't hate her."

"That's just psychological bull—"

"Check yourself." Matt's voice held a warning.

Paul stood to pace the room. His eyes grew huge and wounded, and anger boiled just below the surface, threatening to erupt. Tears spilled over to run down his face, and he swiped at them, embarrassed. "I *won't* call her. You can't make me call her."

"Now, Paul—"

"Just leave me alone!" He spun and rushed down the hallway. His voice echoed back off the walls. "I don't want to talk about it anymore!"

Matt groaned when the front door slammed, and Paul's shoes pounded the deck. He winced as something on the porch toppled over—most likely a rocking chair—and clattered down the stairs. Matt tossed the papers he was holding across the cluttered desk and slumped in his chair. How could this boy he'd become a parent to only a few months ago make his heart ache as if it were being torn apart? And what was he going to do about it?

Matt stood, grabbed his coffee mug, and stalked to the front porch. The night was cool and still, the scent of wild onions a promise of spring. Stars glittered in a moonless sky. The workshop was dark, but Matt knew Paul was huddled in the loft, in sawdust and hay, sorting through his emotions. He set his coffee mug on the porch rail and gathered the toppled rocking chairs before settling into one. The steady back and forth motion soothed. He'd give Paul half an hour to calm down and collect his thoughts, have the good cry he didn't want Matt to see. Then he'd go to him, comfort him, and together they'd sort through the mess.

11

"Hello, stranger."

The voice, smooth and silky, startled Matt. The hammer grazed his thumb, missed the nail he meant to drive into the bottom of a piece of two-by-four frame. He glanced up and his breath hitched. Even in faded jeans and a loose white T-shirt, Caroline was the prettiest thing he'd ever seen. Hair cascaded down the length of her back in a caramel wave gathered by an elastic band. And those honey eyes...he could easily drown in them.

"This is a nice surprise." He scrambled to his feet, brushed sawdust from his shirt, and wiped sweaty palms on the thighs of his jeans.

"Sorry I startled you." She stood in the grass while sunlight danced over her. "Paul told me how hard you've been working the past few days, and I thought I'd bring you some lunch, offer a little help."

"Sounds great. Where's Callie?"

"Andie took her up to the barn to show her how to groom the horses and muck out the stalls. She's going to spend the day. Paul was there when I dropped her off. I guess he's going to help with the stalls, too."

"Yeah, he mentioned that this morning. I could really use his help here, but I knew he needed some time to blow off steam. He's been struggling the past few days, and Andie always seems to have a way of calming him down, getting his head back on straight."

"I noticed. The two of them are very close. It's...sweet."

"Sure." He scratched his chin, frowning. "As long as things stay G-rated."

"Oh, I wouldn't worry too much about that." She set a small cooler in the grass and walked over to where he'd nearly finished the framing. She ran a hand down a two-by-four, smiled. "I love the sweet, clean smell of lumber. It reminds me of my grandfather. He made custom furniture, and sometimes I sat in his shop and watched."

"Well, this doesn't look like much yet, but just give me a few more days. It'll shape up nicely."

"I'll bet the afternoon sun will fall beautifully here. Mrs. Harrigan can curl up like a lazy cat and read to her heart's content."

Matt drew a nail from the tool pouch strapped to his waist and sunk it nicely into the two-by-four with one swift blow. "So, how did you find me? I mean, how did you know I was here today...now?"

"Paul told me." Caroline found another hammer in the toolbox. "He gave me directions."

"Little sneak. No dessert for him tonight. He shouldn't have told you. You have enough to take care of at your own place."

"Nonsense. You've done so much for me. Let me do just a little for you."

"I'm surprised you could get Paul to talk." Matt pulled his notes from his back pocket, checked a measure, and then reached for another two-by-four. "He's been tight as Fort Knox lately."

"I noticed." Caroline watched as he marked the board with a carpenter's pencil, then used the skill saw to make a quick slice through the wood. "He wandered into my office after school yesterday, plopped down on the couch and just sat for a while. He didn't say much, but it was obvious something's weighing on him. I just about had him talking when a parent showed up for a scheduled conference, and I had to cut things short. So, what's going on?"

Matt sighed and set the saw down. He reached for a bottle of water, took a swig.

"It's his mom." He brushed a forearm across his brow. Sawdust drifted from his hair. "She called a few nights ago, said she might come for a visit. Paul hasn't seen her in months. It's really set him off."

"That's a long time to go without seeing your mom." Caroline picked up the wood he'd cut and set it into place. "How's she doing? With the rehab, I mean?"

Matt shrugged as she tapped a nail into the board. "Hard to tell for sure. She says she hasn't had a drink in over two months, but I've heard that before."

"Paul's scared. I don't blame him, Matt." She turned to face him. "He's made a life here with you. A good life. He's afraid that's going to be taken from him."

"I know. It's been weighing on me, too. I just want to do what's right for him. It's hard to discern in situations like this. Eydie's my sister, and I know she's his mother, but..."

"I understand." She knelt down and rummaged through the oversized, metal toolbox at his feet. "What else can I do to help here?"

"You've already done what I needed most." He smiled and brushed a stray hair from her brow. The sweet honeysuckle scent of her shampoo mixed with sawdust and sunshine, like a breath of fresh air.

"Do you have more nails?"

"That can wait." He took her hand, pulled her up to face him. He placed a palm gently on each side of her face, locking his gaze with hers.

"Matt?"

"Hush," he whispered. "Let me."

He leaned in and felt her breath warm on his neck. Though his heart pounded with need, he kept the kiss gentle, no more than a brush of warm lips. Her hands slid to the nape of his neck, fingers twined in his hair. Her touch sent a pulse of heat up his spine.

He wanted more...so much more, but he stepped back, released her.

"I'll get you those nails now." He walked away, had to, before he took her in his arms again and kissed the breath from her. "You blush real pretty, Caroline." He tossed a wicked grin over his shoulder. "The rosy color compliments your honey eyes beautifully."

She gaped, a single finger pressed to her lips. He gathered an armload of two-by-fours and a handful of nails and focused on the frame under construction. Right now, he needed something, anything, to keep his hands and mind busy.

☙❧

Caroline lounged on the couch, her legs tucked beneath her. Soft lamplight spilled over the novel in her lap. She'd read the same sentence three times, and still failed to absorb the words. Her mind kept wandering to Matt, to his calloused, tender hands on her face, his warm lips brushing hers. The kiss had been brief, gentle, barely more than a whisper. Yet it stoked a yearning in the pit of her stomach, sent heat from the tips of her toes clear through the top of her head. She smiled, gave up on the book, and reached to switch off the lamp.

Footsteps on the porch startled her. Warmth fled, and a flash of chills swept through her. Just outside the window, someone stumbled in the dark. An explosion near the steps had her on her feet, heart racing. "What in the world?"

She hurried to the front window, carefully pulled back the curtain and peeked into the moonlit yard. One of the jumbo ceramic planters she'd filled with a colorful mix of wave petunias and propped beside the front door had toppled down the stairs and shattered.

A shadow crossed the darkness and tumbled into a second planter, knocking it over with a resounding crash.

Blood rushed through her ears and the room spun. Wildly, she searched for protection, came up with a fireplace poker. If she hadn't been so terrified, she might have laughed at the cliché.

She flipped on porch lights, then floodlights. The front yard lit up like high noon.

"Who's there?" She stood back from the door, her throat tight with fear, hands trembling. "What do you want?"

More stumbling, another ear-shattering crash as a rocking chair toppled and bounced down the stairs.

"I'm calling 911," she warned.

"Don't!"

Caroline's breath caught. Though slurred and disoriented, the voice was familiar. She dropped the fireplace poker and rushed to open the door.

"Paul!" She dropped to her knees beside him. He

sprawled face-down across the doorway, covered in potting soil, surrounded by shards of shattered ceramic pots and trampled wave petunias. "What happened? Are you OK?"

"No!"

His response turned her blood to ice. "Let me see." Carefully, she rolled him over to find his eyes were huge, the pupils dilated. Blood stained his forehead where broken glass had sliced through skin. "Paul, you're hurt. Talk to me."

"Help me, Caroline."

Caroline choked and frowned as the odor of stale alcohol slapped her face.

"You've been drinking! You're drunk. Oh, Paul, no!"

He tried to shake his head, but gagged and vomited on the cushioned welcome mat instead.

"Nice going. Does Matt have any idea where you are, or what you've been doing?"

Matt...he's going to be furious...and heartbroken.

"Don't tell him," Paul pleaded. He rolled to his side and clutched his gut.

"I have to tell him. He's probably worried out of his mind." Caroline kicked the soiled welcome mat out of the way. "Get up." She grabbed Paul under the armpits, and with great difficulty hauled him to his feet. She ignored his heavy moans, the acute distress in his eyes. "Let's get you into the house. Hold onto me."

Somehow she managed to drag him to the couch, and dropped him there while she went for a trashcan. She returned with it just in time to watch him shudder and heave again as his body tried to relieve itself of the poison.

"I'm dying." His face was ashen, his lips pasty

white.

"Oh, no you're not. Not yet, at least. That may change when Matt gets a hold of you."

"Ohhh!" He slid down the couch, curled his lanky form into a ball as his moans filled the room. Caroline prayed Callie would sleep through it, wouldn't wake and wander down to ask questions.

Caroline knelt beside the couch. Gently she bathed the gash on Paul's forehead with cool water. A bit of pressure quickly staunched the flow of blood, and his moans soon eased to agonized sighs. As she covered the wound with a bandage, his eyes slid closed, and his breathing steadied as sleep took over. Caroline held vigil until she felt comfortable leaving him long enough to phone Matt.

She took a breath, chose words carefully, and whispered a fervent prayer before dialing the number. Boy, this was going to hurt Matt. And she'd do anything not to hurt him. But her hands were tied on this one. She made the call.

"This is a nice surprise." Matt sounded so relaxed, so...cheerful. She hated to shatter his calm.

"It's a surprise, yes." Caroline's voice was clipped. Her hands still trembled. "But nice...no."

"You're upset. What's wrong?"

"It's...Paul. He's here."

"How? He's supposed to be with Andie and Kyle. Andie's barrel racing tonight out at the fairgrounds. Paul went to watch."

"I don't know anything about that." She paused, her heart heavy. She struggled for the right words. "Matt, Paul's been drinking."

"What?" In the background she heard chair legs scrape against the tile floor. She imagined him pacing the room. "You must be mistaken. Paul would never touch the stuff. Not after what he's seen with Eydie. No way."

"I'm sorry, Matt. It's no mistake." Caroline fought to steady her voice. She drew a deep sigh and continued. "He stumbled across my front porch, took out two planters and a rocking chair. I'm not sure how he got here, but he's passed out on the couch."

"Oh, Caroline..." She heard the hitch in his voice, the utter disbelief. "I'm so sorry. I'll be right over."

"No!" The word held more force than she intended. She checked her tone, eased it down a notch. "I mean, he's safe now, and sleeping. Just leave him for tonight. I'll bring him to you in the morning."

"But, Caroline—"

"Please, Matt. I feel like this is...partly my fault."

"Oh, no you don't." His voice held a hint of anger. "Don't go there."

"But he'd already come to my office once, and then Andie came to me again this morning to tell me he was still pretty upset over his mom. She was afraid he'd crack and do something reckless. She asked me to talk to him and I meant to, but I told you my appointments ran over. By the time I was free he'd already left school." She lowered her voice, her throat tight. "I should have made more of an effort, juggled my schedule a bit for him. I let Paul down. I let Andie down, too."

"You did no such thing. Paul did this. He'll take full responsibility, and the consequences."

"You're angry."

"You'd better believe I'm angry."

"Let him stay here tonight, Matt. You can deal with him in the morning. That will be soon enough, and give us all a chance to calm down."

His silence told her he was weighing her words. She waited, held her breath.

"All right. But I'll expect him here first thing in the morning."

"I promise, Matt. He'll be there."

"Call me if anything changes."

"I will."

She hung up and slumped into a chair. What on earth had possessed Paul to act so irresponsibly, so dangerously? He might have stumbled into the pond and drowned, or passed out in the road. He might have—

The phone rang, startling her. She grabbed the receiver before the shrill woke Callie.

"Caroline?" Andie's voice was tight and strained with tears. "Have you seen Paul?"

"He's here. He's OK."

"Thank God. I need to talk to him."

"He's sleeping, honey."

"At your house? Why?" She hesitated, then choked, "He got drunk, didn't he?"

"Why do you think that, Andie?" Caroline's heart raced. "How did you know?"

"Because he rambled about his mom this morning, and he said if she doesn't care what happens to him, why should he." Her voice cracked on a sob. "But *I* care about him, Caroline."

"I know you do, honey."

"I saw him hanging around after school. I'll bet I know where he got the beer. Matt will want to know."

"I'm sure he will. But we can deal with that tomorrow. Paul's had a rough night, but he's going to be OK."

"I was so scared." Andie caught her breath. "He was supposed to come by the fairgrounds, but he never showed up. Kyle and I searched all over. I was afraid to call his house, 'cause I had this feeling Paul was somewhere he shouldn't be, and I didn't want to get him in trouble."

"I think he's managed to do a fine job of that all on his own."

"Does Matt know he's with you, that he's OK?"

"I just spoke with him."

"Paul's in the doghouse for sure. No more car. No—more—life." The sobs came now with a vengeance. "Will you tell him I called?"

"As soon as he wakes up."

"Thank you for helping him, Caroline. Thank you so much."

৵৵

Across the dew-kissed pasture, Matt rocked on his back porch beneath stars that seemed to mock his distress. The chair swayed wildly as he fought the urge to rush over to Caroline's, haul Paul out of his mindless slumber and shake some sense into him.

Why did he do this? Matt longed for an explanation. He bunched his hand into a fist, pummeled the chair's arm. Caroline was right, he needed time to cool off, calm down, find his bearings.

He knew months before Paul finally ended up on his doorstep that the kid needed him. Eydie was headed down a destructive path, and it was just a matter of time before things imploded. But Matt had been on his own road to self-destruction—mired in grief following Mandy's...and their child's...death. For months he'd considered no one's needs but his own, and now he felt like a failure. It shamed him.

He rocked harder, and prayed it wasn't too late to give Paul the stability and guidance he longed for, and desperately needed.

Morning would tell.

෧෮

Caroline woke to heavy groaning. She rubbed sleep from her eyes to find Paul struggling to sit up.

"Good morning, sunshine." She slid from the recliner and went to him. "How's the head?"

He pressed a palm to his belly and grimaced. "I think I have the flu."

"You do, if it comes in a six-pack."

"Oh." He slumped against the cushions. "Oh, no."

"Oh, yes."

His eyes were shadowed with remorse. "Caroline, I feel sick."

"You should. Here's the trashcan." She handed the plastic bin to him. "I hope your aim is better this morning than it was last night."

"Ohh..." He touched the bruise on his forehead and winced. His skin was gray with nausea. "Where's Uncle Matt."

"At home, just waiting to get his hands on you."

"He's gonna be so mad." His eyes filled with tears. "Caroline..."

"I wouldn't blame him if he is." She forced back sympathy and leveled him a look. "You scared us both to death. Why did you do it, Paul?"

"I..." He avoided her gaze, covered his face with a throw pillow. "I don't know."

"I won't accept that. Try again." She threw her hands in the air and paced the floor, anger flaring. "You stumbled onto the front porch and broke my pretty planters. I thought you were a prowler. I had the fireplace poker. I was ready to whack you with it! By the time I realized it was you, you'd fallen and cut your head, nearly passed out across the doorway."

"Please, Caroline, don't shout."

"I'll shout if I want to," she cried, but eased it down a notch. "I had to phone Matt and tell him you were passed out on my couch. Do you know how hard that was...how much it hurt him to hear that?" She pulled the pillow away from Paul's face. "Look at me and tell me, why did you do it? Why did you drink...whatever you drank, until it made you so sick you couldn't even walk?"

"You wouldn't understand." He swiped tears from his cheeks.

"Try me."

He kicked the trash can and it toppled over. His eyes, red and shamed, found hers. "I wanted to know how it feels to be...drunk. I just wanted to know how it feels."

Caroline considered his words for a moment. "And how does it feel? Pretty good?"

"No!" He shook his head, and the movement caused him to wince. "It's awful. I feel so sick, and I don't just mean my head and my stomach." He covered his face with his hands. "But I wanted to know why."

"Why?" Caroline tossed the pillow back onto the couch. "What do you mean?"

"I had to know." He sniffled and swiped his nose, then his eyes on his forearm. "Why she'd rather drink than have *me*." The words were thick, pained. "I wanted to know what's so great about getting drunk that my mom would choose it over...me." He was suddenly sobbing, his breath coming in huge, painful gasps. He doubled over, wrapping his arms across his belly. "I-I j-just want-wanted t-to know."

"Oh, honey." Caroline's resolve melted. She slid beside him on the couch and drew him into her arms. She pressed his bruised head against her shoulder and rocked him gently. "It's going to be OK."

"No. It's all wrong. I feel so bad. Uncle Matt's gonna kill me. I'm so stupid. I let him down."

"You made a mistake. There will be consequences, for sure. There always are. But no one loves you any less. Not Andie, who called last night, by the way, frantic because you stood her up."

That elicited another groan.

"Not me, and especially not Matt."

"I need to see Uncle Matt." Paul pulled back from her and struggled to his feet. "I need to tell him I'm sorry."

She glanced out the front window. Dawn was just spreading a patchwork quilt of color over the horizon. "We have a little time. You'd better clean up first. You smell like..." She wrinkled her nose. "Well, you reek. And a couple aspirin might not be a bad idea, either. I'm sure you'll get an earful when I take you home. If you think your head's throbbing now, just wait."

అఇ

Matt heard the car before it turned into the drive. The wheels spit gravel like shrapnel across the dew-covered grass. Caroline lowered the windows as he walked over. Paul slumped in the seat. He avoid Matt's gaze.

"Matt!" Callie struggled from her booster seat as he neared the car. "Can I stay and play?"

Despite his exhaustion, his heavy heart, Matt leaned through the window to give her freckled nose a quick tap. "Hi, sweetie. You can't stay to play right now, because Paul and I need some time alone to talk. But I'll come over later and bring you a little surprise, OK?"

"OK." Callie pressed her hands against his rough, unshaven face and lifted her head to kiss his cheek. "My daddy used to feel like this."

Her touch, the innocent words, nearly undid him. His breath hitched and he struggled to keep his tone light as he slid back from the window to glance at Caroline. Her honey eyes were shadowed, yet her easy smile soothed his raw nerves and took the edge off the headache biting the bridge of his nose.

"Thank you," was all he could manage before he turned and strode away with Paul at his heels. His mind reeled.

Lord, help me. Give me the right words. Help me to stay calm.

In the living room, Matt's stomach lurched as Paul huddled in the corner of the couch like a dejected puppy. He had the height of a man, was beginning the journey into manhood, yet his heart, his emotions, were still that of a child. It was a difficult place to navigate.

Matt drew a breath, dropped to Paul's level. He was careful to move slowly, not to startle. Fists and threats, shouting and accusations, were not the answer. Paul had endured plenty of that in his young life. So

Matt reached for him and felt sickened when Paul flinched in response.

"It's OK. I'm not going to hurt you." At the gentle tone of his voice, Paul went slack. "I'm angry, disappointed, confused. But I'm not going to hurt you. Maybe ground you for the rest of your life, take away the car keys for a while, give you time to think about what you've done, the danger and stupidity of it, but I won't lay a hand on you—ever."

"I'm so sorry." Paul crumpled. He pressed his face into Matt's T-shirt and wrapped his arms tight as if he'd never let go. "I won't ever do it again. I promise, Uncle Matt." His tone was so genuine, so sincere, it brought tears to Matt's eyes. The lecture he'd planned, all the synonyms for foolish, reckless, thoughtless, dangerous, died in his throat. He held Paul, rocked the child growing into a man, and knew somehow, some way, everything would be OK.

છ∼જી

Caroline grimaced as she drew the Old Maid. No chance of winning the card game now. Callie was on a mean streak, three wins in a row.

"Mama, Matt's here." Callie threw down her cards and hopped from the porch steps to race across the front lawn. Her blonde curls fanned out like a cape behind her. "And Paul, too!"

Matt parked the truck and climbed out. He gathered Callie into his arms and swung her around until she was breathless. Then he set her down and patted her blonde curls. "Hello, sweetie. Long time, no see."

Callie tilted her head. "But I just saw you this morning."

"Was that you? I thought it was your twin."

"I don't have a twin." She propped her hands on her hips and stared up at him. "Hey, you're foolin' me."

"Caught me." He tapped her nose. "Look on the seat in the truck. I brought you something."

She scrambled around him to peek through the driver's door. "Pizza!"

"Can you carry it inside? I'll be there in a few minutes. I want to talk to your mom."

"I can do it. I'm strong." She flexed her arms.

"Yes, you are." He gave her tiny bicep a squeeze, then turned to Caroline and motioned to the cards strewn across a wicker table. "Old Maid, huh?"

"Yes, and I'm losing. Again."

"Well, that's just not right. You don't look anything like an old maid."

Paul fidgeted beside Matt. She turned to him.

"Feeling better?"

He nodded slightly. His eyes were dark and shadowed, and the cut on his head would leave a bruise. "I'm really sorry, Caroline. I'm sorry I scared you last night, that I demolished your front porch." The planters were still strewn across wood planks in shattered bits and pieces. "I'll clean up the mess."

"Apology accepted. The broom's right over there."

"Here." He drew a fistful of rolled bills from the pocket of his jeans and handed them to her. "This should cover the cost of the plants and planters, a new doormat, too."

She met Matt's gaze, saw the conviction there. Consequences were tough sometimes, but necessary. She took the money. "Thank you, Paul."

"I guess I'll get started…cleaning up the mess I made." He heaved a sigh of relief, then took the broom and started to sweep. The *whoosh, swish* of bristles gathering ceramic filled the air.

"We'll be inside when you're finished." Matt said. "We'll save you some pizza."

Matt followed Caroline through the living room and into the kitchen, where he reached for her. "Thank you, Caroline." He pressed a hand to her cheek. "Thank you for taking care of Paul last night. Thank you for your compassion."

"You're welcome." She leaned into him. "Is everything OK now?"

"We had a long talk, and Paul called Eydie. She said she'd wait a while to come down, give him some time to adjust to the idea and her some time to be sure she'll stay firm on the right path."

"That's good." She turned to take glasses from the cupboard, then reached into the refrigerator for a pitcher of lemonade. "I think you need some time, too."

"Maybe...yes."

She filled the glasses. "How's the work on the solarium coming along?"

"Paul and I just put the finishing touches on it. Nothing like the banging of a hammer and the roar of a circular saw to make a hung-over kid think twice before getting loaded again. His head should keep pounding into next week." He took the glass she offered. "Anyway, Mrs. Harrigan will be home tomorrow, and Jim's like a kid on Christmas Eve."

"Hmm...that's so nice." Caroline drew a sip of lemonade.

"Come here." Matt took her glass and set it on the counter beside his own. He pulled her close, kissed her forehead, her lips. "Thank you for your help, Caroline.

I couldn't have finished the project on time without you."

"My pleasure." She smiled, basking in the scent of his clean aftershave, and pressed her cheek to his soft cotton T-shirt with a sigh. "I enjoy spending time with you, Matt."

"Who knows." He kissed her again. "Maybe one day I'll build a solarium for you."

12

The wail of an ambulance siren sent chills up Caroline's spine. Unlike the city, sirens were rare in Mountainview. She glanced up from the flowerbeds along the front of the house that she was pruning to see the ambulance scream by, lights flashing, sirens blaring. Her heart caught in her throat. Someone was hurt.

Through the open living room window, the phone rang. Caroline's heart missed a beat. She dropped her trowel.

"I'll get it, Mama." Callie tossed her jump rope aside and raced into the house. The soles of her sneakers slapped wildly through the living room. A moment later, she came bounding back with the cordless phone, breathless. "It's Paul, Mama. He says he needs to talk to you right away."

"OK." Caroline peeled off gardening gloves. Clumps of musky earth plopped into the pile of weeds she'd collected. The siren continued to wail, the sound no longer fading. *It's close, just beyond the pasture.* She took the phone from Callie. "Paul—"

His voice was a rising wave. "I need you to come get me. Uncle Matt's hurt. They're loading him into an ambulance—"

"Ambulance!" She stumbled over the word.

"Hurry. The paramedics are pulling out. They're

leaving me here!"

"Where are they going?"

"I don't know. County General, I think."

"I'm on my way!" She dropped the phone into the pile of weeds and struggled to her feet. "Callie, get in the car." She raced into the house, grabbed her car keys, her purse. Her heart pounded. Blood rushed through her ears, drowning the sound of the siren that wailed back toward them and then faded into the distance.

"What's wrong, Mama?" Callie was frozen in place when she returned to the front yard. She stared with wide, frightened eyes.

"Matt's had an accident. We have to get Paul, then head to the hospital right away." She placed a hand on Callie's back and nudged her toward the car. "Hurry, honey."

Her hands shook as she strapped Callie into her booster seat. She forced them steady as she shoved the key into the ignition. The engine roared to life, and she backed blindly down the driveway. Neatly-edged grass, trimmed by Matt just yesterday morning, blurred as she picked up speed. All she could think of was Matt in an ambulance...racing to the hospital. Hurt.

"Mama, slow down!" Callie wailed, clinging to her booster. Caroline forced herself to breathe, to obey some semblance of the posted speed limit as she sped toward Matt's house.

When they arrived, Paul paced at the foot of the driveway. He didn't wait for her to come to a complete stop before he opened the door and leapt in. His eyes were red and swollen, his face ashen. "Please hurry, Caroline."

"What happened? Is Matt OK?"

"I don't know." He slapped the thighs of his faded jeans. "He was up in the workshop loft, fixing some of the floorboards. I noticed they were loose the other night when I was up there, and I mentioned it to him." Tears pooled in his eyes. "It's my fault, Caroline. I went up there the night my mom called. I wanted to be alone, and Uncle Matt stays away from there. He'd have never known about the boards if I hadn't said anything. It's all my fault."

"It's *not* your fault. Matt makes it his business to know what needs to be repaired. He would have noticed the boards eventually, anyway."

"A section collapsed and he fell through. He must have slammed his head on the concrete. I don't know how long he was lying there. I couldn't find him when I got home from track practice, and I thought maybe he was working on one of his projects. He does that sometimes in the evening when he's got something on his mind he's trying work through. That's when I found him crumpled on the floor. He was out cold and bleeding...so much blood all around him." Paul trembled. "I couldn't wake him up!"

Caroline summoned every ounce of strength, gripped the steering wheel as though it were a lifeline. She felt lightheaded and cold deep in her bones.

Make me strong, Lord. Matt needs me.

"Mama, is Matt gonna die like Daddy did?"

"No!" The word was harsh. Callie bit a trembling lip, and Caroline instantly regretted her tone. "Honey, everything's going to be OK."

She didn't know that, not for sure. But she had to say something, and if she said the words, maybe they would become real.

"But Daddy had an accident, and then he died."

"His accident was different, honey—not like Matt's at all."

Paul choked. Caroline feared he might be sick. She forced her own tears back as the road blurred. Words jammed in her throat. There was nothing more to say.

The emergency room wait felt like an eternity. A muted TV mounted to the far corner of the room near the ceiling flashed the same tickertape of headline news. Callie snuggled on Caroline's lap, sobbing. There was no consoling her, but finally, the sobs wore her out, and she fell into a fitful sleep, much to Caroline's relief. Paul huddled a few chairs away, lost in his own grief, his head buried in his hands. Caroline didn't even try to coax him out of his silence.

In the hallway, tennis shoes squeaked over polished tile.

"Caroline!" Sue rushed through the lobby doors, her face a mask of concern. "I got here as fast as I could. Any word yet?"

"No. But, how did you know?"

"Kevin's a police officer, remember? He heard the call come over the scanner and phoned me right away."

"Oh." Caroline shifted Callie in her lap, trying to relieve the pressure on her legs. Her voice sounded hollow. It seemed to echo inside her head, as if coming from a distance. She felt cold. So cold. "I think it's bad, Sue. No one's come to talk to us yet. It's killing me, not knowing."

Sue dropped into a chair beside her. "Tell me everything you know."

"I'm worried about Paul." Caroline gnawed a fingernail. "He hasn't said two words in the past hour."

Sue frowned. "I'll have Andie call him. She'll get him to open up." She pulled out her cell phone, quickly tapped a text message and hit send. "I'll wait with you until the doctor comes to tell us something."

Fright tore into Caroline with the thought. She glanced around the room, noted drab-gray hard plastic chairs and racks of dog-eared magazines that had been fanned through by countless visitors. The odor of bleach mixed with window cleaner stung her sinuses. There was an undercurrent of sweat, fear, and the constant, annoying swish of doors down the hall opening and closing.

Please, Lord, let Matt be OK.

"Do you want to pray?" Sue asked, as if reading Caroline's mind.

"Yes...please." Caroline pressed Callie to her shoulder. Together the women bowed their heads.

Sue's voice whispered across the room, her tone filled with the solid, deep friendship she shared with Matt, borne of the many celebrations and heartaches Caroline knew they'd shared over the years. The prayer soothed like a balm to her nerves. She felt a measure of warmth chase the chill from her bones.

Another long hour passed before a doctor strode into the room. He was clad in crumpled mint-green scrubs, and his wrinkled face was stern, his eyes serious as he cleared his throat.

"Mrs. Carlson?"

Caroline leapt to her feet and rushed toward him. She let the assumption that she was Matt's wife slide. If it meant access to Matt, she'd let the doctor assume anything he wanted.

"How is he?" She felt lightheaded, her heart

suddenly pounding. Blood rushed through her ears like a tsunami.

The doctor drew a heavy sigh, which Caroline took as a bad sign. "We've run several tests. Your husband..."

My husband? The room went gray for a moment, and dancing black spots formed a veil before her eyes. *Curt? No, he means Matt.* She stumbled back and placed a hand on the wall to steady herself. For a breathless moment, she was overcome with confusion. She struggled to focus on what the doctor said.

"...has a concussion as well as some swelling in his brain, which is not so unusual following a ten-foot fall onto a concrete surface. I can't give you a definite prognosis. We'll just have to wait and see. He's unconscious. The next twenty-four hours will be critical."

Critical. Dear Lord, help him.

"I...I'd like to see him."

"Me, too." Paul leapt to his feet. The doctor took one wary look at him and shook his head.

"He's in the Intensive Care Unit. I'm sorry, but no one under eighteen is admitted back there."

"But I have to see him!" Paul took a step forward, ready to do battle. The doctor held his ground, didn't even flinch. Caroline guessed he'd been in this situation more times than he could count.

"Paul, right now we have to do what's best for Matt." She placed a hand on his arm and struggled to maintain a soothing tone, when inside she was screaming. "I know it's hard, but try...please."

"Paul, come home with me," Sue offered. "Andie's waiting there for you. And we'll take Callie, too. She's been here long enough."

Caroline turned to him. "Go with her, Paul. Please."

"But, I don't want to go!" He crossed his arms over his chest, bowed up to his full height. "You can't make me, Caroline."

She sighed. "No, I can't. But I'm asking you to please do this. Help Sue with Callie. She's going to be scared when she wakes up. She'll need you." Caroline delved into her purse and removed her house key. She pressed it against Paul's palm. "Get her a pair of pajamas and some clean clothes for school. And she'll want her baby doll." Tears sprang to Caroline's eyes. "And check on Socks, make sure he has plenty of food and water. Will you do that for me, please? I'll stay here with Matt, and I promise to call you right away if anything changes."

Paul's gaze locked with hers as he clutched the key in his clenched fist. A heartbeat or two passed before he offered the slightest nod, then turned. "Here, let me take her," he said quietly to Sue. He bundled Callie into his arms. "I'll carry her to the car."

❧❦

The ICU room was stark and dreary beneath unnatural fluorescent lighting. Bathed in the eerie glow of lights, Matt lay unconscious in a bed surrounded by *whooshing* and beeping machines that seemed to mock her with their repetitive symphony. His breathing was light and regular, his pulse carefully monitored.

Caroline touched the thick, sterile bandage that covered his head and kissed dusky smudges beneath eyes that were just beginning to blacken from the fall. He looked like a prizefighter who'd lost...badly.

Waves of heart-wrenching memories washed over her, and she sank into a stiff plastic chair beside the bed.

"Oh, Matt." She reached for his hand, mindful of the IV needle and tubing, and twined her fingers with his. "Please, be OK."

As tears flowed, Callie's words rang through her mind. *Is he gonna die, Mama? Daddy had an accident and he died. Is Matt gonna die, too?*

"Ma'am?"

The voice startled her, and she turned to see a bespectacled older nurse who carried herself with an air of authority. Earlier, she'd brought Caroline a pillow and blanket and a lukewarm cup of coffee from the nurse's station. Her eyes, though weary, were filled with compassion. "Can I get you anything—water, more coffee, a snack?"

Though her throat was parched, Caroline shook her head. Her stomach roiled, and she knew she couldn't keep anything down. "No, thank you. I'm fine."

I'm beginning to fall in love with Matt. The words plowed through her, knocked her back in the stiff chair like a punch to the gut.

But she couldn't fall in love with him. She wouldn't. If she loved him, God would take him, just like He'd taken Curt. *And I can't survive so great a loss a second time.* She thought of Callie losing her Daddy, and realized with a stab of shock that over the past weeks Callie had begun to view Matt as a father figure.

What if suddenly Matt's gone? How will Callie's fragile heart cope with a second devastating loss?

What was she *doing*? What on earth had she been *thinking* to allow this to happen? She *couldn't* have feelings for Matt. The stakes were too high to chance. She'd spent the past year easing her heart back onto stable ground. She couldn't risk losing it again.

She had to protect Callie, protect herself. And there was only one way to accomplish that.

I should go. I should leave right now, this minute, before I'm in way too deep.

But I can't. I promised Paul I'd stay here. I promised. I'll just sit here and wait. I don't have to feel anything. I won't feel anything.

And when Matt's out of the woods—if he's ever out of the woods—I'll go then. I'll just get up and walk out.

I can do that. I can.

Tears scalded Caroline's cheeks as her heart broke in two. Better a broken heart, she thought, than two shattered lives.

❧

Caroline marked time by the oversized digital clock on the wall above Matt's bed. There were no windows in the ICU, so she had no idea whether it was light or dark outside, sunny or storming. She was in a time warp, and the minutes seemed to stretch endlessly before her.

She drifted in and out of sleep, dozing restlessly in the uncomfortable chair. Nurses wandered in at different intervals to check on Matt. One thought to bring her a cup of tepid coffee and crackers pilfered from the nurse's station. Caroline sipped the bitter brew, her mouth dry and scratchy as sandpaper, and cocooned herself in a cotton blanket. She studied Matt, watched the steady rise and fall of his chest, and listened to his even breathing. The rhythm comforted.

He continued to sleep in some far off place, and the thought that she might never see his deep blue eyes, hear his gentle voice, brought on another round of tears. She thought she'd cried the well dry when she lost Curt, but that anguish had only been the beginning.

Voices whispered down the hall and medicine carts whirred over bleached tile. Monitors *whoosh-hissed* and *tick-tick-ticked* in a steady cacophony. Caroline's eyes felt heavy. Thoughts drifted and swirled like a dark funnel cloud. She tried to gather them, make sense of them, but everything was jumbled. She sighed, tucked her cheek against her clasped hands, and slept.

෧෬

Deep, guttural moans filled her dreams. Matt's fingers twined tight with hers, and her eyes flew open.

"Matt?" Her legs tingled with sleep as she stood to lean over the bed. She ignored the irritation and placed a hand on his chest to calm him. His heart thumped a steady rhythm beneath taut chest muscles. "It's OK. I'm here."

She choked on a sob. *Thank you, Lord, for bringing him back.*

"Caroline?" His eyes fluttered open. He squinted against the light as he surveyed the room, dazed. "Where am I? What—what happened?"

"You fell, Matt. In your workshop—yesterday."

"Yesterday?" His blue eyes, swollen and ringed purplish-black, registered confusion. Caroline brushed her fingers along his stubbled cheek.

"You don't remember?"

He shook his head. The slight movement elicited a groan. His skin went ashen. "My head..."

"Try not to move. You have a concussion."

"Paul?" he managed. "Callie?" His voice drifted, and his eyes were like two dark stones set in pasty clay.

"They're with Sue and Kevin. Paul's OK. They're both OK. Just rest now, Matt."

He drew a shaky breath and grasped her hand. His fingers were cold, and she massaged the calloused tips to warm them. "Don't go, Caroline."

"Hush. Sleep." She pressed a finger to his lips and leaned to kiss his bandaged forehead. Tears rolled down her cheeks. She didn't have the heart to tell him she'd already left.

❧❦

Matt spent three days in the hospital. He could have used a few days longer, but as it turned out, the nurses had to fight to keep him down that long. Caroline was convinced the entire staff threw a huge party the day he was released.

Matt Carlson did not get the Best Patient Award. Not by a long shot. Caroline knew this for a fact, because she'd been at his side the entire time, fighting the battle of wills right alongside the nurses.

She'd never forget the look on Paul's face when she drove up with Matt in tow late that afternoon. The engine was still running when he leapt from the steps, flew across the grass, and tore open the passenger door. He threw his arms around Matt, his eyes clouded with tears.

"Whoa." Matt's arms trembled as he hugged back.

"It's good to see you, too."

"Your eyes..." Paul stepped back, winced at the bruising. "Hurt bad?"

"Like an elephant kicked me, but I'll heal. Help me out of here, OK? Things are still a little fuzzy."

Together, Paul and Caroline helped him into the house. He settled on the couch, and Caroline tucked a faded patchwork quilt around his shoulders.

"Promise me you'll rest today." She shook a finger at him. "No tools and no going into the workshop, OK?"

"Yes, ma'am." He tried to wink, grimaced instead through swollen lids.

"I'll keep an eye on him, Caroline. Don't worry." Paul stood beside her like a panther ready to pounce. "He won't get by me."

"Your refrigerator is well-stocked," Caroline said. "Just about everyone from church has sent over a dish, so you're in no danger of starving."

"Mrs. Harrigan made frosted fudge brownies," Paul added. "I saved you one, Uncle Matt."

"One, huh?" Matt kicked off his shoes, and adjusted the pillows under his bruised, stitched head. "And how many did you plow through?"

Paul shrugged. "I dunno."

"Can't count that high, huh?

Paul grinned, clearly relieved to find Matt's sense of humor still intact. Caroline's heart tugged at their exchange. She knew she had to get out of there quickly, before she changed her mind and decided to stay. She fished an amber vial from her purse and set it on the coffee table.

"Your pain pills," she said. "In case the headache becomes unbearable."

"It's OK now. It's dulled to a low, throbbing bite. I can deal."

"Well, just in case..." She turned and started toward the front door. "Is there anything else you need before I go?"

Matt reached for her, pulled her to him and brushed roughened knuckles gently across her cheek. "Thank you, Caroline."

She took a step back. He'd indulged in a shower just before his discharge from the hospital, and the woodsy scent of soap was intoxicating. His eyes narrowed with confusion, and she struggled to maintain distance, both emotionally and physically. "You're welcome."

"You OK? You were awfully quiet on the ride here."

She gulped hard, threw on a poker face, and steadied her voice. "Just a little tired." It wasn't a lie, really. She felt dead on her feet. Every breath was strained. "I really have to go now. Callie's waiting at Sue's for me."

"OK." He was clearly wounded by her rush to leave, and her heart felt bruised, too. She managed a limp smile, though she felt as if she was dying a thousand deaths. The screen door slapped against its frame as she left. She barely made it to the car before the tears came.

13

Caroline threw herself into tending the front flowerbeds. The sweet fragrance of spring filled the air, and she felt edgy with energy. Maybe ripping out the offensive weeds and adding some color to the damp earth would lighten her mood. Since Matt's accident, she felt dead inside. She hadn't seen him in nearly a week, had barely spoken to him except for quick daily calls to check on his condition and to see how Paul was managing.

She missed him...and she didn't know what to do with the feeling. Try as she might, she couldn't just tuck it away and forget about it.

"Hey, Caroline." The voice startled her, and she turned to see Paul lope across the grass, his tall, lean form framed by warm afternoon sunlight. "You attacking the dirt?"

"Guess you can say that." She stood and brushed soil from the knees of her jeans. "Thought I'd plant a flat of pansies, maybe some begonias to add a splash of color to the front of the house."

"Cool. That'll look nice."

"What brings you this way?"

He jammed his hands into his pockets and shrugged. "Just felt like walking, had to clear my head a little. Do you mind?"

"Of course not." She peeled off her gardening

gloves, dropped them on the ground. "Come in and have something to drink. I just made sweet tea."

"OK." He followed her up the steps and into the living room. "I saw Callie at Andie's barn. She's getting to be a pretty good little rider."

"I know." Caroline glanced back over her shoulder. "Andie's been great with her. Who would have guessed my little city girl would have a thing for horses?"

"Andie had her walking barrels. She said I was distracting them, so I got kicked out of the paddock."

"Sorry about that."

"Uncle Matt kicked me out, too." Paul sighed. "Said I've been hanging around the house too much, worrying about him. He told me to take a hike, get some fresh air."

Caroline eased the ache in her heart by filling glasses with tea and arranging chocolate chip cookies on a plate. "How...is he feeling?"

"A whole lot better. He got the stitches out yesterday, and the doctor said everything is healing OK, so he can go back to work in a few more days." Paul took the glass Caroline handed him, drew a long swig. "I got to drive him to the doctor's office. It was pretty cool. And I drove to church yesterday, too. We missed seeing you and Callie there."

"Oh..." She hesitated. "I let Callie sleep in. She's been worn out from...everything."

"Yeah, well..." He fidgeted and carefully avoided her gaze while he took a cookie from the plate. "I guess I should get back home. I gotta keep Uncle Matt from trying to get up on the roof or something crazy. He doesn't sit still very well."

"So I noticed when he was in the hospital."

Paul emptied the glass with a final, long gulp and set it on the counter. "Caroline, are you OK?" His words came out in a rush.

"Me? I'm fine."

"Really?"

"Of...of course." The words burned like lye. She pasted a smile on her lips. "Why?"

He shrugged, his eyes full of questions. "I just figured, maybe you're mad at me or something."

"Why would I be mad at you?"

"I was pretty rude to you that day...in the emergency room, I mean. I was scared, and I said some things…"

"Nonsense. You weren't rude. You were just torn up. We all were." She placed the tray of cookies on the table. "Everything's going to be OK, though."

Paul shrugged. "I just thought maybe you haven't wanted to come around, you know, to see Uncle Matt since he's come home because you're mad at me."

"No. Never." She shook her head and brushed dark, shaggy hair from his face. "I'm not mad at you, Paul. It's just...grown-up stuff, complicated. Nothing for you to worry about."

"Well, OK." He seemed unconvinced as he reached for another cookie. "Do you still want me to come by this Saturday and hang those shelves in Callie's playroom?"

"Sure, if Matt doesn't need you to help him with anything."

"No." He bit into the cookie and brushed crumbs from his lips. "He's meeting with some big wigs from city council about a downtown development project they want him to manage. He doesn't need me for the planning part. I just help with the hard labor." His quirky, lopsided grin made Caroline laugh. It was the first time she'd relaxed in days and it felt good.

"I guess I'll see you on Saturday, then." She filled a baggie with a half-dozen more cookies and handed it to him. "Take a few for the road."

"Mama, what's Heaven like?" Callie asked as she dressed her baby doll in a delicate pastel pink sundress and matching bonnet. She'd been asking a lot of questions about Heaven lately, confirming that Caroline had made the right decision in distancing them from Matt. Callie had obviously been deeply affected by his accident.

"I don't know, honey. I haven't been there yet."

"Julianna says the streets are chocolate fudge, and the stars are made of sugar, and that all you do is play games and eat candy and then play some more. And there aren't any chores, and you never have to take a bath. Do you think she's right, Mama?"

Caroline drew Callie close, breathed in the sweet scent of apple shampoo mixed with the chocolate pudding she'd had for dessert. "I think that's a question for Pastor Jake."

"But how can I ask him when I haven't seen him in forever? We didn't go to church on Sunday, or yesterday, either."

A stab of guilt sliced through Caroline. She'd avoided Sue all day at school, too. Not wanting to fib her way out of going to choir practice, she'd simply steered clear of her friend to avoid giving some lame excuse. Now the guilt of skipping practice and letting down the choir, as well as denying Callie, consumed her.

"We'll go on Sunday, honey."

"You promise?"

Just then the phone rang, sparing Caroline. Callie raced to grab the receiver.

"Hello?" She was so proud of her newfound telephone skills. She savored every opportunity to test them. "Oh, hi, Matt! How's the big boo-boo on your head?...Really?...Ouch, that must've hurt!...Sure, I'll kiss it...I miss you, too...Yeah, Mama's right here...OK, I will..." She pressed the phone into Caroline's hands. "Matt wants to talk to you, Mama."

Caroline's limbs went suddenly cold, as if an arctic blast had swept through. She wanted to talk to Matt more than anything, but she shouldn't. It wouldn't solve anything. It would only tear open the wound she'd been trying desperately to staunch for the past week. But she couldn't *not* talk to him. Not with Callie shoving the phone at her, eyes bright and expectant. Caroline took the phone, cleared her throat, and summoned her most matter-of-fact voice.

"Hello, Matt."

"Hi, Caroline." The sound of his voice, so calm and soothing, was salve to her nerves. "I'm glad I caught you."

"Actually, we're just getting ready to leave. I have to run and get some...light bulbs." *Light bulbs? Where on earth did that come from?*

"Oh." The hesitation in his voice made the flimsiness of the excuse all too clear. Caroline cringed inside. "Well, I was wondering if you'd like to bring Callie over tomorrow and have dinner with Paul and me. We're both...missing you."

"I can't." She answered a little too quickly. "I have

to...weed the flowerbeds." *Weed the flowerbeds?* "I didn't get to finish them the other day." At least that much was true. She'd been interrupted by Paul's visit, and hadn't felt like pulling weeds after he left. The knowledge that he'd carried guilt over her keeping a distance nagged at Caroline. So she'd taken Callie to town, ordered pizza—stayed busy to chase the guilt and loneliness away.

"Oh." Matt hesitated. "I...understand."

"I have to go. I'm glad you're feeling better. Good-goodbye."

"Car—"

She hung up before he could get the word out, tossed the phone on the couch as if it held a deadly virus.

"Mama, I don't want to pull weeds!" Callie cried. "I want to go see Matt."

"Well, we can't."

"Why not, Mama? Why can't we go see him?"

"Because...because..." She floundered for an answer. "Because I said!"

"That's not fair!" Callie ran from the room, sobbing. Her sneakers pounded the stairs and she slammed her bedroom door. The vibration shook Caroline. She gaped, stunned by the sudden outburst. *I'm losing her, too.* As Callie's sobs filtered down the staircase, Caroline sank to the couch and hung her head.

❧❦

"The shelves look great." Caroline ran a hand over the polished teakwood planks mounted above Callie's toy box. Paul had spent the morning measuring, leveling, carefully installing, and the results were nothing less than beautiful. "I love what you've done here. What a great idea." He'd installed a length of shelving around the perimeter of the room, about eighteen inches below the ceiling.

Paul's blue eyes shone. "I figured Callie could perch all her stuffed animals up there, kind of like a display."

"Good thinking. All this shelving is going to be just perfect for Callie's toys and games. Now I don't have to worry about tripping on something and breaking an ankle."

"Thanks, Caroline. Uncle Matt showed me how to hang shelves." He collected his tools, placed a screwdriver and tape measure neatly into the toolbox she'd seen Matt use on several occasions. "You know, the more I do this, the more I think I might like to build things for a living when I get older."

Caroline handed him the level. "Why wait until you're older? You're doing it right now–building, I mean—and quite well, I might add. You could print some fliers and get them out in the community. I'm sure there are lots of people who can use help with small projects and fixing things around their houses. And it sure beats bagging groceries."

Paul closed the lid on the toolbox and stood to face her. He looked more like his uncle every day, with his muscles filling out and gaining definition. The thought of Matt filled her with longing.

"I guess you're right. Uncle Matt said he started building things in high school, too. He said his dad— my grandpa—showed him how, so I guess we're kind of carrying on a tradition of sorts. I think that's pretty cool."

"Yes, it is." She was dying to ask him about Matt. *How is he, what's he doing now that the wound on his head has healed?* But she bit back the words.

"Mama, can I..." The words died on Callie's lips as she bounded into the room and discovered Paul's handiwork. "Wow! Oh boy!"

"Hop up, munchkin." Paul hunched down and tapped his shoulders for Callie to climb aboard. "I'll hand your zoo of stuffed animals up so you can put them on the shelves the way you want, OK?"

"Yeah." Callie clamored up his back and wrapped her legs over his shoulders like a little monkey. With Paul's height, her head nearly brushed the ceiling. She squealed with delight when he tossed a stuffed bunny up to her.

Caroline smiled wistfully as she watched them work together. Paul was going to be a good father one day. Matt was teaching him well.

"Mama, Mama, wake up."

Caroline groaned and rolled over. She shivered as Callie tugged the blankets off her and they fell to the floor in a tangled heap.

"Mama!"

"It's too early to get up, honey." Her mouth felt dry, her eyes too heavy to pry open. "Go back to bed."

"No, it's not." Callie poked her shoulder. "It's Sunday, and you promised we'd go to church today. I wanna go, Mama. I need to ask Pastor Jake about Heaven and the chocolate streets and stars made of sugar."

Sunday. Ohhh...

"Mama!"

"Stop shouting, Callie. You're going to wake the entire town."

"Uh-uh. The birds are singin' and the sun's shinin', too." She pulled the curtains back and sunlight filled the room. "Everyone's up but you."

Great. Wonderful. Coffee...I need a good, strong cup of coffee. Or two.

Caroline hadn't slept through a single night in over two weeks. She'd barely slept at all—except for this morning. And now Callie was standing beside the bed, already dressed in her cornflower blue dress with her favorite black patent-leather shoes and white-lace ankle socks. She'd even brushed her hair and clipped the curls to one side with a barrette.

"Will you make pancakes, Mama? With chocolate chips? You don't make them as good as Matt...or Daddy, but that's OK. I still like them pretty much."

Caroline sighed, stretched. "Sure, I'll make you pancakes. Just give me a minute here to get my motor going."

Callie laughed and handed her the pale pink terrycloth robe she'd tossed at the foot of the bed last night. Caroline shrugged into it and cinched the belt tight to ward of the morning chill.

"I promised Paul I'd sit with him and Andie today, Mama. And Matt's gonna be there, too. Yeah, yeah, *yeah*!" She twirled, the dainty blue dress swirling around her knees. "I miss him *so* much."

Caroline's heart lurched, and her breath hitched in her throat. The room went suddenly hot...sweltering. She loosened the robe. "Callie—"

She stopped spinning to gaze at Caroline with innocent eyes. "What, Mama?"

The words died in Caroline's throat. "N-nothing, honey. Go take the pancake mix from the pantry and set it on the counter with the milk and butter. I'll be right there, OK?"

"Yes, Mama."

As Callie skipped from the room, the heels of her patent leather shoes echoed on the wood floor, leaving a path of scuff marks. Caroline fought the overwhelming urge to flop back on the bed and curl up in the safe cocoon of her blankets. How on earth was she going to manage this...this morning in church? How was she going to look at Matt, *see* him, and not let on how miserable she felt?

She pattered to the bathroom and splashed water on her weary face. She'd pull herself together — fast. She had no other choice.

❧❧

Though his head was bowed in silent prayer, Matt smelled the light, familiar scent of Caroline's perfume and knew she'd slid into the seat beside him. He finished what he needed to say, took a deep breath, and opened his eyes. And his heart caught. She was beautiful in a hunter-green floral-print dress that set off a mass of thick, caramel curls.

"Caroline..."

"Hello, Matt." The look on her face startled him, and a smile died on his lips. Her mouth was set in a rigid line, and she deftly avoided his gaze. Winter on Mount Everest could not have been more frigid.

"How are —"

Suddenly, Callie bounded over Caroline and launched herself into his lap. "Matt, oh, Matt!" She threw her arms around his neck and kissed his cheek. She smelled of chocolate and maple syrup. "Mmm, you're smooth today."

"Hi, sweetie. My, oh my. You sure are a sight for sore eyes."

She crinkled her nose at him. "You smell good. Can I see your boo-boo?"

"Sure." He dipped his head, revealing the wound that was nearly healed. Soon, the whole incident would be no more than a bad memory.

"Does it still hurt? Do you want me to kiss it? Mama always kisses my boo-boos to make them feel better."

A hint of blush eased across Caroline's cheeks, and Matt gave an inward groan at the thought of her kissing away his pain.

"It doesn't hurt anymore, sweetie, but thank you for offering." All that hurt right now was his heart, from trying to figure out what was going on inside Caroline's head. He studied her, sitting stiffly in the seat, as if she might shatter into a million pieces at the slightest touch. "Your mom sure looks pretty today."

"I know. I picked her dress. She couldn't decide so I helped her. It's my favorite."

"Well, you have very good taste." He nodded. "I like it, too."

Through the service, Callie sat tucked between them, holding tightly to Matt's hand with Paul and Andie seated on the other side. If it weren't for the strained look on Caroline's face and the way she leaned away from him as if he were the worst sort of poison, he might almost believe they could be a family.

A family? The thought startled Matt. *Where in the world did that idea come from?*

෴

If Caroline didn't know better, she'd say they almost looked like a family with Callie tucked neatly between them.

A family? The thought startled Caroline. *Where on earth did that idea come from?*

She shouldn't have dawdled so long at the house. By the time she and Callie arrived, the only seats left were right up front—near Matt. And of course, Callie demanded to sit with Matt. Caroline had every intention of slipping away as soon as the service ended. Matt smelled of sawdust and pine and soap. She tried not to breathe.

"Caroline..." Matt reached for her hand following Pastor Jake's benediction. "We need to talk."

"There's...nothing to talk about." Callie tugged the hem of her dress. "Mama, can I go with Andie? She wants to give me another riding lesson. Paul's gonna come, too."

"Not today, Callie. We need to go home."

"But, Mama—"

"I'll drive her, Caroline." Sue ambled over. "I've got some work to do at the barn, so I'll be there with the kids."

Caroline gulped back embarrassment. How could Sue still smile at her when she'd blown off choir practice with Easter just two weeks away?

"I-I don't want to inconvenience you."

"It's no inconvenience. I'll bring Callie home to you in time for dinner, OK?"

"But—"

"Please, Mama. *Please!*"

Callie's eyes were huge with longing. Caroline's resolve shattered.

"OK, honey. You can go." She nodded to Sue. "Thank you." She drew Callie into an embrace, kissed the top of her head. "Be good, OK?"

"I will, Mama."

As she watched them go, Matt reached for her hand.

"Caroline, come for a drive with me."

"No, Matt."

"Whatever it is, whatever's on your mind, I can't help you if we don't talk about it."

"I don't want you to help me."

"Then help *me*." His blue eyes were deep as the sea, imploring. "Help me understand what's going on here. I give. I call uncle. I'm pathetically clueless as to what you're thinking…feeling. But I want to understand, Caroline. I really do. Please help me. Take a drive with me. Let's talk."

14

"Smells like summer," Matt took her hand, eased her gently into the truck. "There's nothing better than the scent of fresh-mowed lawn after a long, cold winter." He went around the front of the truck, slid into the driver's side. "Hungry?"

"No." She could barely fathom eating. A tight knot tugged her stomach. She leaned on the passenger door, leaving a chasm between her and Matt as he eased the truck into gear.

"Careful. You lean on the door any harder, you might fall out into the road."

"What?" She eased up on the door a bit. "Oh, sorry."

"You act like you're afraid of me."

Her chin came up. "I'm not afraid of you."

"Oh, well..." His gaze swept from the road to her, then back, like a tennis ball in a heated match. "Caroline, did I say something or do something to offend you when I was in the hospital?"

"What? No. Of course not."

"It's just that I don't remember very much from when I was there, just a lot of fuzzy darkness, and I thought...maybe—"

"No."

"I do remember your gentle voice, the touch of your hand soothing the bruises that blackened my eyes, the painful stitches in my head." His voice was thick, husky with emotion. "It...helped."

She brushed his words aside. "I did what anyone would. That's all."

"Hmm..." Matt cleared his throat and trained his gaze on the road. "Paul told me he put up some shelves in Callie's room."

"He did a great job."

"He's been working on some fliers to post around town, thinks he might get some offers for a handyman special. You have anything to do with that?"

"Maybe."

He fumbled with the radio, found the local easy-listening station. A soft melody soothed raw nerves. "Well, it's a good thing I found a car for him. Sounds like he might need it."

"He told me...that you found a car, I mean."

"It's not much more than a hunk of dinged metal, but Paul thinks it's 'pretty cool'."

"To an almost-sixteen-year-old, anything on four wheels is pretty cool."

"We're going to fix it up together." He slowed the car as they neared a bakery. "Are you hungry? Sweets soothe the soul. Maybe a slice of pie?"

"No, thanks." He might as well ask her to devour a mountain. "I'm not hungry."

"Feel like walking? The river walk looks nice today."

Caroline followed his gaze. Tulips bloomed in a colorful trail along the cobblestone path and gentle ripples of water danced along the surface of the river. A warm breeze coaxed through the passenger window. "OK."

She waited while he swung the car into a parking

space and killed the engine.

He eased from the car and came around to open the door for her. "Sue told me you were offered a fulltime position at the high school next year."

"Yes." She slipped on a soft cotton sweater as they started down the walk. "The principal spoke to me about it Friday."

"That's great, Caroline. And Callie still likes school?"

"She loves it." The heels of her pumps clicked against the walk. "She's the only kid I know who doesn't want summer vacation to come."

"Amazing." Matt grinned and shook his head. "You can always send her to summer school."

"Actually, there's a summer reading program at the local library. Callie's already signed up."

Matt paused to look at her and sunlight framed him. "I miss this, Caroline... talking to you. I miss it." He reached for her hand, but she drew back and crossed her arms.

"You shouldn't miss it. You *can't* miss it."

"But I do." His gaze was troubled. A heartbeat, then two passed while birds sang in the dogwoods that lined the walk and sunlight glinted like diamonds dancing on the river.

Caroline's belly roiled as she hugged her arms tight across her chest.

"I can't see you anymore, Matt." The words tumbled out.

"You can't—what?"

"I can't see you." Her throat was suddenly thick and tight. Her eyes burned, and she wished desperately for sunglasses to shade them, to hide the tears. "I can't do...this."

"This?" His eyes seemed to deepen like turbulent blue-gray ocean waters. "Caroline, whatever it is...whatever I've done—"

"I told you, you haven't done anything!" She turned her back to him.

"Talk to me. Whatever's troubling you...please let me in." He eased behind her, his breath warm on her neck. "I want to be your fortress, Caroline. I want to be the one you run to when you're hurting, when you're scared, when you...need. Let me be that person."

"But you can't be!" She choked on the words. Until now she'd been convinced her heart was already broken. But somehow, some way, it shattered into a million more fragments.

"I don't understand. I thought—"

She turned to face him. "Please, Matt. Just let it go. Let *me* go."

Instead of the anger she'd expected, his voice gentled and coaxed. "What are you afraid of, Caroline?"

A lump blocked her throat. Molten tears burned her eyes. She murmured, "I'm afraid of you, Matt."

"Me?" His eyes widened like two blue pools. "Why on earth are you afraid of me?"

A chill crept deep into her bones. "I'm afraid of loving you, Matt. It scares me to death."

"Oh, Caroline." The breath rushed from him. He pressed a hand to her face. "It's OK. Really, it's going to be—"

"No! It can't be OK. Not this time. Please take me home." She stepped back. "I want to go home. I need to think this all through."

"Sometimes you can think things to death, Caroline." His gaze was bruised. "Sometimes you just have to go with things...let them happen."

"Maybe you feel that way, but not me." She crossed her arms and lifted a quivering chin. "If you care anything about me at all, Matt, just take me home."

$\approx$ $\approx$

Matt rocked beneath the light of a crescent moon. The night was cool, the air crisp and resplendent with the scent of lilac and mowed grass. In the distance a cow moaned.

Matt remembered how Mandy loved sitting outside in the evening to gaze over the moonlit mountains as they talked about their day. He missed it...the closeness, the sharing. Life had been good until he'd gone and ruined it.

Like he'd ruined things with Caroline. And he wasn't even sure what he'd done, or how to fix it.

"Mind if I sit with you?" Paul called through the screen door.

"Come on out." Matt motioned to the empty rocking chair beside him. "Take a load off. It's a nice night."

"Yeah. There must be a gazillion stars." Hinges squeaked, and the screen door slapped against its frame. Paul slid into the rocking chair and pulled his ball cap low over his eyes. "It's weird to think they're the same stars I'd see in the city if I was still there."

"You miss it?"

"Nah. Not one bit."

Matt laughed softly. "Four months ago you would have given your right arm before admitting that."

"Things change. I...love it here now."

"Love it?"

"Yeah."

"Why?"

Paul shrugged. "I dunno."

"Andie?"

"She's part of it," Paul admitted. "She's...a good friend."

"Just a friend?"

Paul rocked the chair as if he was racing for the lead in the Indy 500. "Well...maybe more. Who knows?"

Matt grinned. "Way to dodge a question. You must take after your uncle."

"Which one?"

Matt burst into laughter.

"It's good to hear you laugh." Paul slowed the rocking to a cantor and slouched in the chair. "You haven't done that in a while."

"Not much to laugh about when your head's split wide open."

"That really freaked me out, Uncle Matt—seeing you out cold, in a pool of blood. I thought you were..."

"Dead?"

He shuddered. "Yeah. I've never been so scared."

Suddenly a floodlight flashed on in Matt's head. Scared...dead...Caroline afraid of him...running scared.

"What are you grinning for?" Paul looked positively mortified. "I just said I thought you were...dead."

"I love you, Paul. You just gave me a piece of the puzzle—a huge piece."

"What puzzle? What are you talking about?"

"Never mind."

Paul shook his head. "Grown-ups," he huffed.

"Just when I think I'm starting to understand them they go off and get all weird again."

Matt smirked. "Sorry to break it to you, but you'll be a grown-up one day, too."

"Just get me to sixteen and I'll be happy. I want to drive."

The night whispered as darkness deepened. Matt knew by the way Paul tugged and twisted a frayed thread of denim at the knee of his jeans that he had something else on his mind. So he waited patiently, because experience told him the words would eventually surface.

Paul sighed. "I need to tell you something,"

"I'm all ears."

Paul linked his fingers together, cracked his knuckles, then adjusted the ball cap again. "Uncle Matt, I love it here because...you make me feel safe and...um..."

Matt knew the words came with great difficulty. Paul held his emotions inside a fortress, and the walls were just beginning to crumble

"And...I feel wanted, even when I do the stupidest, most thoughtless and selfish things." His gaze, a deep blue echo of Matt's, was imploring. "I don't want to leave. I don't want to go back to the city."

Matt sighed and squeezed Paul's shoulder.

"I can't promise that will never happen. It's up to your mom, you know that. But I *can* promise you I'll do my best to do what's right for you."

"I-I know you will." Paul's gaze locked with his. "I trust you."

I trust you. Those three small words spoke volumes. If Matt could win over a misguided, mischievous, bitter, scared kid who'd been beaten down more times than he could count, surely, with a little patience, he could do the same with Caroline.

15

"Hand me that wrench." Matt motioned to the toolbox beside the car.

"This one?" Paul hoisted the tool for Matt's inspection.

"Yeah. Now, watch what I'm doing."

Paul scooted his head beneath the front hood as Matt gave the wrench a twist. "What's that?"

"The carburetor. It's what's sputtering. If it happens again, you'll know what to do."

"Cool."

Matt closed the hood and tossed Paul a set of keys. "Let's see how she runs. Crank her up."

"Oh, man!" Grinning from ear to ear, Paul dove into the driver's seat. He slid the key into the ignition, and the car growled to life. "Listen to that. She roars like a tiger."

"Just keep the tiger tame, OK?" Matt leaned in the passenger window, checked the engine lights. "This car looks good on you. Want to take her for a spin?"

"You bet I do."

"Let's take a ride into town. There's something I need to get."

৵৵৵

"Mama, guess what?" Callie gushed as they drove

home from school. "I got picked to be in the talent show."

"You did? That's wonderful!"

"I'm gonna tell a story with illus-illus—"

"Illustrations?"

"Yeah. And I've been looking through books for ideas. Mrs. Brabson said that's called brainstorming."

"Yes, it is."

"Will you come and watch me perform?"

"Of course I will. When is the show?"

"Friday afternoon."

"That's just a few days away. We'd better brainstorm fast."

"I know, Mama." Callie tapped the side of her head. "I already have lotsa ideas."

Caroline turned into their drive and gasped. Flowerbeds along the front of the house bloomed with a waterfall of color. Fiery-red begonias, smiling pink pansies, and wave petunias in the brightest lilac hue danced over the moist earth along the front of the house.

"Mama, Matt was here." Callie clamored from her booster seat and sprinted up the walk. "Look, he left his gloves."

Caroline slipped from the car to follow Callie. She recognized the stained leather. Matt had worn the gloves the day she'd helped him with the Harrigan's solarium. She picked them up and inhaled the scent of soil and sweat. "I guess he did."

"Hey, maybe Matt will come to my talent show."

Caroline's heart tugged. "Honey, I don't think—"

Callie picked a pansy and offered Caroline the smiling bud. Sweet spring filled the air with promise. "He'll come, Mama. I'll pray about it, and Matt will come."

⬥⬥⬥

Friday afternoon brought a rush of activity. Two students dropped by Caroline's office to ask her to sign college admission forms. Then Mrs. Conroy, the mother of a pregnant teen she'd counseled, came in teary-eyed. The tears had quickly led to hysterics, and as Caroline listened, her heart broke for lost dreams and unfulfilled hopes.

The clock ticked off the hour, and the talent show at the grammar school was underway. Caroline's pulse quickened, and her blood pressure rose. If she didn't wrap things up quickly, she'd miss Callie's debut.

"Mrs. Conroy, forgive me but I really must go." She reached for her purse. "I'll walk you out, and we can talk again on Monday if you'd like."

The woman sniffled all the way to the parking lot, where Caroline tucked her into the driver's seat of her car. "Is three o'clock on Monday OK?"

"She's only sixteen."

Only sixteen. Paul was nearly sixteen, and Andie. *How would I handle it if they were in the same situation?*

"Here's my home number, Mrs. Conroy. You can call this weekend if you need to talk, OK?"

"Thank you." She dabbed her eyes with a tissue, then tucked the number into her purse. "Thank you so much."

The grammar school auditorium was packed. Caroline leaned against the back wall and glanced over the program she'd grabbed as she walked through the door. Callie was the last to perform. Still two acts to go.

She scanned the room. Cameras flashed as proud

parents on the front row snapped pictures of their little singer. Beside them, his gaze trained to the stage, sat Matt. Her heart leapt into her throat at the lean line of his shoulders and waves of charcoal hair.

Matt turned, saw her, and tapped the empty chair beside him. She wove through the crowd and settled in.

"Hi," he murmured.

Caroline merely nodded and clasped her hands in her lap. The scent of sawdust mingled with soap and, despite her best efforts, she felt her pulse quicken.

Callie appeared through a fold of maroon, velvet stage curtains, lugging an oversized sketch pad. She was dressed in her favorite pink polka-dotted skirt with her blonde curls pulled into a bushy ponytail and tied with a baby blue ribbon. She propped the oversized sketch pad on an easel beside the microphone and opened to the first page.

Wide, bright eyes swept the audience, and a huge grin lit her face when Matt winked and nodded, then lifted his camera to snap a photo. Caroline grimaced. She was in such a rush that morning she'd forgotten the camera.

"Once upon a time..." Callie's sweet, innocent voice filled the auditorium as she related the story of a little gray kitten with snowy-white paws who'd lost his family but found a new one to love. She shared the kitten's great adventures chasing mice and sleeping at the foot of a soft, warm bed with a little girl who read him storybooks. And she told of his friends, a mama with long, caramel hair who sang like an angel, a strong man who fixed broken things around the house and shared yummy pizza, a boy who painted colorful murals on the walls, and a girl who rode a horse named Stormy like she was sailing on the wind.

By the time she finished and took a dramatic bow, Caroline was a quivering mound of tears. The crowd's applause was thunderous.

Matt reached for the camera bag slung over the armrest of his chair as the auditorium emptied. "Let's go record this moment."

"Mama! Matt!" Callie raced down the auditorium aisle and flew into Matt's arms. He lifted her high and swung her around while she squealed with delight. "Did I do OK?"

"You did awesome." Matt handed her a single pink rose. "As a matter of fact, you did such a great job I'd like an autograph."

"Wow!" Callie kissed his cheek. "Am I a famous author now?"

"Well, to me you certainly are." He fished in his pocket for a folded slip of paper while Caroline found a pen in her purse and handed it to Callie. Callie bit her lower lip as she printed her name. "Thank you." Matt said when she handed the autograph to him. "I'll treasure it forever." He folded it carefully and tucked it into his wallet.

"Take our picture, Mama." Callie snuggled against Matt's leg.

Caroline took the camera, aimed and focused. Through the viewfinder, she saw clearly Matt's love for Callie. The tenderness in his gaze turned her insides to jelly.

Principal Jenner paused as she passed by. "Here, I'll snap a photo of the three of you together."

The jelly in Caroline's belly turned to granite. "No, that's not necessary."

"C'mon, Mama." Callie tugged her close until the

three of them were snuggled together. Her sweet apple shampoo mixed with the woodsy scent of Matt's aftershave. "I want a picture for my scrapbook. Andie's gonna help me make one."

Caroline relinquished the camera and slid close to Callie as Matt lifted her into his arms.

"There you go. That's nice." Marian trained the lens on them and Caroline plastered a smile as if it was the most natural thing in the world to pose there in the school hallway like a family. The camera flashed once, twice, three times before Marian stepped back, satisfied.

"You told a wonderful story, Callie." Marian reached into her tote bag. "Here's a special certificate for a job well-done."

"Thank you." Callie took the certificate. "Oh, it's so pretty." The border was edged in shiny gold stars.

"Well, this is certainly special." Caroline admired the certificate. "We'll have to get a frame and hang it on the wall in your bedroom."

"Matt can do it." Callie wiggled from his arms. "I'm hungry, Mama. Can we get some pizza for dinner?"

"Sure, honey. That sounds good."

"You come too, Matt. I'll show you my drawings. There's one of you and Paul and Stormy. She's galloping with Andie in the saddle."

Matt glanced at Caroline, then bent to Callie's level and placed a hand on her shoulder. "I'm sorry, sweetie, but I can't go with you this time. I've got to get home. I promised Paul I'd help him with a project for school. But I'll see you again soon, and you can show me your drawings then, OK?"

"You promise?" The light went out of her smile.

Matt nodded. "Yes, I promise."

"Well...OK." She pressed a delicate hand to each side of his face before tipping his head forward to place a kiss where stitches had knitted into a neat scar. "There. All better now."

Caroline's insides melted. She pressed a fist to her mouth to stifle a sob and turned away.

రెండు

"Callie, get down off the mower. You're going to fall and get hurt." Caroline whisked her safely to the ground.

"But Mama, I like to pretend I'm driving."

"You can pretend to drive in another ten years. Right now I'm just trying to get this motor started." She lifted the hood of the riding mower Aunt Nora had left in the shed and gaped at the engine, not sure what came next. "Paul will be here any minute to help with the lawn, and he certainly can't cut grass without a working mower."

"I'll help cut the grass, Mama. I'll go get my scissors."

"Have at it." Caroline grinned wryly. Trimming their expansive lawn with a pair of blunt-tipped scissors would keep Callie busy for...well...the next decade, at least. "And take Socks with you. He's prowling around my feet."

"That's 'cause he likes you, Mama."

"Well, he won't like me very much when I step on him."

"Oh, no." Callie scooped up the cat. "He wouldn't like that at all."

"And stay away from the pond." Caroline called

as Callie skipped away. "If I catch you anywhere near it again, you'll be grounded from the library for a month."

"Grounded from the library? Can't you come up with a better threat than that?" The gruff voice startled Caroline, and she smacked her forehead soundly on the mower's gearshift. Matt's face came into focus through a brilliant flash of stars.

"Ouch!" The blow knocked her to her knees. "That-hurt-a-lot!"

"Sorry." Matt rushed over to press a hand to her head. His gentle touch soothed the pain away and brought on a torrent of emotions. "I didn't mean to scare you. Are you OK?"

"Yeah, sure." The world tilted and went dark for a moment. "Nothing a little ice and a generous dose of aspirin can't cure. What are you doing here, anyway?"

"Good to see you, too."

She pressed a finger to her forehead where a goose egg had popped to the surface. "Ouch."

"Let me see." He eased her onto the mower's seat and drew her head against his chest. Gentle fingers slipped through her hair to massage the bump. She pressed her face to the clean scent of his T-shirt and surrendered to his touch. "You're going to have a bruise." His fingers worked their magic. The throbbing subsided. "And, to answer your question, I drove over with Paul. He was itching to take his new car for a spin. He said he's going to mow your yard this afternoon."

She wiggled out of his grasp and stood to face him. "Only if I can get this no good, worthless, piece of junk to run."

Matt laughed. "Let me take a look at it. Maybe I

can get it going."

"Good luck. I've tried everything I know to do. It doesn't respond to sweet talk. Maybe a good kick..." She'd already tried that, too, but was loathe to admit it.

Matt gave her a gentle push toward the door. "I'll take care of this. Go put some ice on that bump and take a look at Paul's car. He's just dying to show it off."

She found Callie perched beside Paul in the front passenger seat while he demonstrated a variety of dashboard gadgets. Music blared from the radio and windshield wipers swished as Callie released washer fluid. Giggles tinkled over the music.

"Nice car, Paul." Caroline leaned into the open passenger window. He'd hung a pine-scented air freshener from the rearview mirror, and the fresh scent clung to the car's interior. "And I see you have a shotgun driver this afternoon."

"That's me." Callie tapped her chest proudly with one hand while she changed the radio station with her other. "Paul says I only have to wait nine more years 'til I can drive, too."

"Thanks a lot, Paul. That's just one more worry to keep me up at night." The horn blared, and she jumped. Her head smacked against the window frame, and began to throb again.

"You wanna drive with us, Mama?" Callie found the air conditioner, blasted the fan on high. Her hair tufted in wild blonde waves.

Caroline rubbed her head, shook away optic stars. "No. You two have fun."

"OK, Mama." Callie opened the glove box, sifted through the contents.

Caroline heard the lawnmower fire up, and Matt rode out of the shed like a cowboy on a bucking bronco. He drove around to the car, then cut the motor's engine while he conferred with Paul. Moments later, Paul turned off the car's ignition, slipped from one side of the car while Callie scrambled from the other, and loped to the shed.

He emerged holding the weed trimmer, pausing just long enough to pull the starter cord so it roared to life. While Matt circled the yard on the mower, Paul trimmed overgrown grass around the trees and along the driveway. The scent of fresh-mowed grass filled the air.

Caroline sighed as Matt swiped sweat from his brow. She couldn't let him and Paul spend the afternoon mowing the lawn beneath the hot spring sun and not at least offer them a meal.

She went into the house to search the refrigerator and settled on marinated chicken, a salad, and mixed vegetables with buttery crescent rolls.

The sun dipped low on the horizon by the time Matt and Paul finished mowing. Caroline had the chicken baked, the table set, and fresh glasses of tea poured. Matt crossed the deck and paused to brush grass clippings from his jeans before coming into the kitchen to wash up at the sink.

"Mmm...smells like a feast."

"Stay for dinner?"

"I thought you'd never ask." He dried his hands with a towel and leaned against the counter.

"Thank you for helping me." Caroline handed him a glass of sweet tea. "How did you get the mower to start?"

"I just gave it a dose of fresh oil and cleaned the filter. It was a little rusty from lack of use."

"Oh. I guess I don't know much about mowers."

Matt swiped a forearm across his brow. "That's OK. You'll learn."

Paul came to the door and stomped grass from his shoes. "You want me to call for Callie? She was just behind the shed chasing Socks."

"I'll call for her. You go ahead and wash up. Dinner's ready." Caroline went out on the porch. "Callie, dinner!" Her voice echoed over the pasture. "Come and eat!"

Paul followed her, and the screen door slapped behind him. "I'm telling you, she was behind the shed. I just saw her."

Caroline strode toward the shed and called again. "Callie, come on in. Dinner's ready."

Matt came up beside her. "No luck?"

"No." She sidestepped as he pressed ahead of her. "She's become more brazen about exploring around here now that she's getting used to the place. I've caught her down near the pond three times this week."

"Callie!" Matt called. He hunched his shoulders and cupped his hands to his mouth. "Callie, answer me!"

The concern in Matt's voice made worry catch in Caroline's chest. "You don't think..." The words died in Caroline's throat. She changed direction and raced toward the pond. Matt rushed at her heels. With his size and strength, he quickly overtook her. His voice ricocheted over the pasture.

"Callie!" They both skidded to a halt at the water's edge. The surface was calm, but impossibly murky. Matt was about to wade in when Paul's voice rang out.

"Here she is!" He came around the corner of the house with Callie on his shoulders.

Caroline sobbed with relief and bolted toward

them. "Callie Grace Lafollette, where were you?"

"Behind the house, Mama. Socks got stuck under the porch. He was cryin' so I crawled under there to get him out." She was covered in dirt, her nose a brownish-gray nub.

Caroline hauled her from Paul's shoulders and set her firmly on the ground. "Don't you ever wander away again."

"I didn't wander, Mama. I was right by the house."

"I *called* you, and you didn't answer."

"I couldn't hear you, Mama. Socks was cryin' real loud."

"You *scared* me." With a sob, Caroline fell to her knees and wrapped her arms tightly around Callie. "Don't *ever* do that again."

❧

"You OK?" Matt took the dish Caroline had washed, dried it and stacked it in the cabinet above the sink.

"Yeah." She sighed as she ran a glass under the faucet and soap bubbles disappeared down the drain. Her eyes teared again.

"Hey, there." Matt shut off the water. He set the glass on the counter and drew her close. "It's OK. It's over and she's fine, Caroline. Callie's fine."

"Can we step outside? I need some air."

"Sure." He led her onto the porch, settled her into the glider. "Better?"

"Yeah." She wiped her eyes. "I'm sorry."

"Don't be. You had a scare."

She gnawed a fingernail as he slid into the seat beside her. The night was still, with clouds blanketing the moon. A storm brewed, and the air smelled of rain.

Callie's laughter spilled from the house as she beat Paul at yet another game of Old Maid.

Matt heard her sudden, sharp intake of breath. "It happened at church."

"What? Oh!" The realization hit Matt like a freight train. She meant Curt. "Church? How?"

"Curt was an accountant. He volunteered to work on the church finances, keep the books balanced and take care of depositing the Sunday collections. One night he went back to the church late to finish up some work. Callie had been invited to attend a young authors' conference the school hosted for students. Even then, Callie loved books, and she'd dictated a story to her kindergarten teacher that she planned to share. "

The glider swayed as she shifted her weight and sighed. "Anyway, after the conference Curt took Callie and me home and then went over to the church to close the books. He was in the office working when..." Her voice caught, and her gaze took on a dazed look as if she was seeing it all over again.

"It's OK, Caroline. You don't have to."

"I want to. I *need* to."

"OK." He took her hand, waited for her to find the words.

"From what I understand, he was finishing up when it happened. The lock on the security door to the parking lot had been broken, but workmen were out to fix it that morning. Curt thought it was fine, but I guess not. He was sitting at the table in the bookkeeping office, tucking cash into the moneybag, when a man rushed in. He demanded the money, but Curt refused. He would never turn over God's money to a thief. He put up a good fight, but the intruder—he overpowered

Curt with a knife."

Matt fought the urge to interrupt, to console her with tender words.

"The custodian was working late that night, too. He heard the commotion and came running. He found Curt on the floor, bleeding and barely conscious. He called 911 immediately, but by the time the ambulance arrived Curt had lost a massive amount of blood." She trembled, drew in a quivering breath. "He was in ICU two days when I left the room long enough to run down to the lobby to see Callie. One of the ladies from church was caring for her, and she brought Callie by the hospital. Anyway, I was only gone from the room for half an hour. But when I got back…"

"Oh, Caroline." Matt's heart ripped for her. He saw the pain in her eyes, the incredible hurt. "I'm so sorry."

"I couldn't stay in Chicago any longer, Matt. So when Aunt Nora gave me the house…I came. It meant a fresh start for me and Callie…away from the bad memories."

"I know." He smoothed hair from the nape of her neck with gentle fingers as he pulled her close and rocked her. "You are so strong, Caroline. I had no idea…no idea at all."

"I'm sorry, Matt…for pushing you away. I don't know how I feel. I'm just…so confused."

He twined his fingers with hers. "I understand. I…loved Mandy with all my heart, just as you loved Curt. But that part of my life…it's over. Loving someone else now doesn't diminish that in any way. It's just…it's life."

"But how can I love *you*, when sometimes I still miss *him*?"

"He'll always be a part of you...a part of Callie. Nothing will ever change that." He stroked her cheek. "The church is having its annual Easter egg hunt and picnic on Saturday. Callie would have a blast, and I'd really like you to go...with me."

She pressed a fist to her lips and nodded. "Yes. I'd like that, Matt...very much."

16

"How many eggs do you think Pastor Jake will hide for us today, Mama?"

"I don't know, honey. This is all new to me. We'll just have to see."

"I think there's gonna be gazillions."

Caroline laughed as she sealed the lid on a cake platter that held the strawberry shortcake she'd baked that morning. "It would take a long time to hunt that many eggs, you silly goose."

"But Mama, I'm a really fast runner. Mrs. Brabson says I might be a track star *and* an illus-illus—"

"Illustrator."

"And an ill-u-stra-tor when I grow up."

"That would be wonderful, honey."

"How much longer 'til Matt gets here?"

Caroline checked her watch. "Any minute. Do you have your Easter basket and a jacket? It's supposed to storm tonight."

"I've got them, Mama. Can I go wait on the porch?"

"*May* I. And yes, you may. Just stay close to the house."

"I will."

As Caroline gathered her jacket, the phone rang. "Hello?"

"Caroline, it's Matt." His voice was strained. "I'm

sorry, but I'm stuck down at city hall. There's been a slight problem with the plans for the project I'm working on and the commissioners called an emergency meeting. I need to get things ironed out before I leave here."

"On Easter weekend? Oh, Matt, I'm sorry. Is it going to be OK?"

"Yeah, but it might take a while. Why don't you and Callie go on to church, and I'll meet you there as soon as I can."

"OK." She struggled to hide the disappointment from her voice. The last thing Matt needed was another worry.

"And Caroline, in case I don't make it before the pie-eating contest starts, tell Callie to cheer loud for Paul. He's had his heart set on winning."

"I will. We'll see you when you get there."

She and Callie loaded the cake and Easter basket into the car and headed to the church. Callie squealed with delight when they turned into the parking lot. "Look at all the people! I see Pastor Jake over by the playground. I wonder if he hid all the eggs yet. Oh, there's Paul and Andie on the church steps. Can...*May* I go see them?"

"Sure. I'm going to set our cake on the dessert table and talk to Sue for a while." Caroline motioned to a long folding table where Sue was busy arranging an array of colorful desserts.

"OK, Mama." Callie ran toward the church, curly pigtails flapping in the breeze. Caroline gathered the cake platter and headed toward the desserts.

"Hi, Sue."

"Well, hello, Caroline. It's great to see you." She took the strawberry shortcake. "Mmm, this smells delicious."

"It's Matt's favorite."

Sue winked conspiratorially. "I might have guessed."

"Would you like some help with the desserts?"

"Please. I'm trying to keep the table intact until the egg hunt is over, but it's a losing battle. Mysteriously, a dozen oatmeal raisin cookies have already disappeared. What a coincidence that Kevin and Kyle both love oatmeal raisin cookies, and that I just caught them prowling around here."

"In that case, I'll pull up a lawn chair. We can manage crowd control together."

They settled in and shared coffee from a thermos while they watched Callie and the other kids chase each other in the cooling afternoon air.

"I haven't seen Matt yet." Sue refilled Caroline's foam cup.

"Oh, he's at city hall fixing a problem with the downtown development project. He should be here soon."

"That's no surprise. Matt's a perfectionist when it comes to building things. If anyone can get a problem straightened out, he can."

"I know. He's sure been a help to me. I don't know how I'd have managed to get Aunt Nora's house put to rights without Matt."

"You mean *your* house. It's your house now, isn't it, Caroline?"

"Yes."

"So you're planning to stay here?"

"I am. And I want to thank you, Sue, for inviting me to sing with the choir. For not biting my head off when I missed practice after Matt's fall. And for bringing me to this church in the first place. Now I don't feel so...lost."

Sue's cornflower blue eyes widened. "Hey, don't thank me. The choir is a whole lot better off for having you in it."

"That's really generous of you, but I feel like I belong here now, and you've been vital to that happening. I don't know where I'd be—where Callie would be—if you hadn't been so kind."

Sue smiled wistfully and squeezed her hand. "God would have found another way. He always does."

Caroline nodded. "You helped Matt, too. He told me so."

"You two have been talking, then?"

"A little. Maybe more than a little..." Caroline frowned and wrapped her hands around the foam cup. The warmth of the coffee soothed her. "I've really hurt Matt. I said some things I wish I could take back."

"Don't worry too much, Caroline. I've known Matt most of my life, and he's pretty tough. He'll be OK. If he cares about you, he won't let go."

ॐ৶

"Mama, may I go see Stormy?" Callie toted a basket full of candy-filled plastic eggs as Caroline helped Sue collect empty platters from the dessert table. The afternoon's festivities were a resounding success, and the crowd thinned as people went home to prepare for Easter morning.

"Where is Stormy, honey?"

"Behind the church. Andie and Paul rode her and Brown Bear here this morning when they came to help Pastor Jake fill the Easter eggs. I'll bet Stormy's lonely,

193

Mama. I haven't gone to visit her all day. She prob'ly needs a hug."

Caroline reached for another platter. "Only if someone goes with you, honey. I can't right now. I told Sue I'd help her clean up."

Andie loped over. "I'll take her, Caroline. She's right. The horses could use some attention."

"OK. But put on your jacket, Callie. It's turning cold."

"All right, Mama."

"Don't be long, OK? It's getting late."

"OK, Mama."

Caroline watched them cross the church playground and retreat around the back of the church. Trees lined the property, and their leaves whispered uneasily in the growing breeze. Beyond, the sky darkened with the threat of rain. She thought about calling them back, but Sue appeared, startling her, and the words died on her lips.

"I really appreciate you helping so much today." Sue took the platters from her. "Let's get inside before the storm hits. Maybe after we're done washing these, we can go over your solo for tomorrow's service...if you're not too tired, that is."

"I'm fine. I'd like that." Caroline followed her into the church kitchen. "And I need the practice."

"Good. It's settled, then."

Sue sang as she worked, and Caroline joined in. The sweet harmony lifted Caroline's spirits as she wondered if Matt would ever arrive.

"What angels make such a beautiful sound?"

"Matt!" Caroline turned from the sink filled with billowy bubbles to find him leaning in the doorway. His eyes were dark with fatigue, his hair disheveled.

But he smiled that terrific smile of his, the one that made her heart melt with longing.

"I could devour a slab of strawberry shortcake right about now. Did you save me any?"

"I might have." Caroline grinned at him. "And there might be a warm, juicy burger as well as a mound of Sue's creamy potato salad along with it. Although I'm sure you don't deserve it one bit since you missed the entire picnic and the lion's share of dishwashing."

He took a step toward her. "I'm so sorry, Caroline. The mayor—"

"Shh." She dried her hands and handed him a plate of food. "No explanation is needed. I'm just glad you're here safely."

Sue placed the last washed platter into the cabinet and drained water from the sink. "The dishes are done. I'm going to check the sanctuary." She gave them a casual smile. "I'll be back."

When she left, Matt turned his attention to Caroline. "Tell me about your day."

"Sure. We can talk while you eat. You must be starved."

"I am." He unwrapped the plate she'd prepared for him. "It's awfully quiet around here. Where's Callie? I figured she'd pounce on me first thing to show off the collection of eggs she amassed during the hunt."

"She's out back with Andie and Paul, visiting with the horses. I'll bet Callie sweet-talked Andie into a short ride around the property."

Matt checked his watch and frowned.

"I just met Andie and Paul crossing Collier Road on horseback. They were headed home to put the horses up because a storm's brewing."

"Oh. Callie was supposed to check in with me when she was done with the horses." Caroline forced back a sense of foreboding that swept through her. "She must have forgotten in all the excitement. I'll bet she's in the library. She saw a book in there earlier that she wants to borrow."

Matt left his plate of food on the counter and followed Caroline into the hallway. Sue was busy shutting off lights down the hall.

"Have you seen Callie?" Matt asked as she flipped another switch, casting the area into darkness.

"Not for the past hour. I just made a sweep of the rooms, and no one's down the hall."

"Did you check the library?"

"Yes. Callie wasn't in there. No one was. The church is deserted except for Pastor Jake and the three of us. Everyone else has gone home."

The first twinge of fear settled in Caroline's gut. She hurried into the sanctuary and switched on the lights. "Maybe she fell asleep in here." She strode the length of the aisle, carefully checking each row of seats. But there was no sign of Callie. Caroline fought back rising panic.

Matt was at her heels. He took her hand. "She must still be out back. Let's go take a look."

Behind the church wind gusted, and the sky grew dark and ominous with the threat of rain. Caroline shivered. She remembered her first night in Mountainview and the terrible storm that had frightened her and Callie. She shouted Callie's name into the wind.

"There's Pastor Jake by the shed." Matt was already heading in that direction. "Maybe he saw something." Matt rushed over to help him haul the church's industrial-sized grill through the shed's double doors. "Have you seen Callie?"

Pastor Jake closed the door and hitched the padlock. "Not for a while. I heard Andie tell her to head back into the church and check in with Caroline."

Caroline scanned the property and the woods beyond. Her heart was tight with fear, her head pounding. Playground swings swayed and a stray foam cup danced in the restless wind. She cupped her hands and shouted again, "Callie!"

"She has to be here somewhere." Matt scanned the horizon. "Don't worry, Caroline. We'll find her. Let's spread out."

Pastor Jake and Sue joined them. They hollered Callie's name as they fanned out to sweep the property. Sue headed back into the church to comb the rooms again while Matt and Pastor Jake moved toward the woods. Caroline searched the parking lot, deserted except for Matt's truck and the three cars belonging to the searchers. Minutes passed like hours.

"Oh, Callie, where are you?" Tears stung Caroline's eyes as she checked the interior of each car and Matt's truck. Perhaps Callie had crawled inside to get warm and fell asleep.

"I just spoke with Paul." Matt clutched his cell phone in one hand. "He's at Andie's, putting up the horses. Andie said she sent Callie in to find you when they left. She said Callie wanted to go with them, that she even tried to come after them as they left, but both she and Paul sent her back and watched her until she got safely inside the church."

Caroline's spine stiffened. She remembered Callie's words. *"I can run really fast, Mama."*

"What is it, Caroline?" Matt's eyes filled with concern. "Tell me."

"Do you think Callie might have tried to follow Paul and Andie—that she went after them when they weren't watching?"

"I don't know why she would disobey them, Caroline."

"She loves those horses, Matt, and she loves to be with Andie and Paul. She probably just didn't realize the danger." Her voice caught. A sob escaped her lips.

Like the pond. She likes to go near the pond. Caroline quaked as the rising breeze slithered around her like a hissing snake. A ripple of thunder vibrated across the sky, and the heavens opened, shooting bullets of rain that quickly grew into a downpour. Darkness covered them like a thick quilt.

"Don't worry, Caroline. We'll find her, I promise." Matt wrapped his jacket around Caroline's shoulders to shelter her from the rain. He touched her chin and lifted her gaze to his.

Sobs choked her, and Matt drew her into his arms. The clean scent of his soft T-shirt and his strong, sure embrace calmed. She pressed her face to his chest, remembering the words he'd spoken not long ago.

"I want to be your fortress, Caroline. I want to be the person you run to when you're hurt, when you're scared...when you need."

She clung tighter when Matt said to Sue, "Call Andie and ask her what route she and Paul took to get home. Pastor Jake and I will retrace their steps. Ask Kevin to round up Kyle and some others to search the roads and the woods." This last command took Caroline's breath away. The trees beyond seemed to swim against an angry sky.

Matt's determined gaze held hers. "Stay here in case Callie wanders back."

He turned from her as she began to protest. "Sue, take care of her for me." And then he rushed toward the woods.

17

Matt phoned to check in an hour later and Caroline's pleas tore his heart.

"Tell me you've found her."

"Not yet, but we will." Matt tried hard to sound upbeat. He was soaked through to the skin and muddy up to his thighs from stomping through overgrown pasture and along the creek that bordered the church's property. He was bone-tired and ravenous, but those needs got pushed aside as he thought of Callie alone out in the cold, stormy darkness. "There are two-dozen men searching now, plus Andie, Paul, and Kyle. It's going to be OK, Caroline."

"But it's so dark and cold, and she's all alone, Matt." Her voice caught on a sob. "My baby's all alone. She must be terrified."

"Let me speak to Sue again, OK?"

"But—"

"Please, honey. Kevin needs me to give her a message."

Matt heard the rustle of static on the line as Caroline handed the phone over to Sue. He waited while Sue walked to the hallway, where Caroline wouldn't overhear.

"How is she?" He asked.

"Holding up as well as can be expected," Sue murmured. "Where is Callie, Matt? Why can't we find her?"

"Only God knows, and I'm counting on Him to lead us to her." He paused and cleared his throat. "Don't say anything to Caroline, but Kevin radioed Sheriff Myers over at the highway department. He thought it best to inform him, just in case. They just issued an Amber Alert."

"Oh, Matt."

"Stay close to Caroline, Sue. Keep her away from the TV and radio. Try to get her to eat something and rest, OK?"

"You know I will."

"We've got the horses. Andie thought it might help to cover more ground if we use them, despite the rain, and I think she's right."

"Be careful, Matt. This storm is a bad one."

"Just take care of Caroline, and I'll take care of things here."

He disconnected and slid the phone back into his pocket. The battery was almost dead. Didn't much matter, the storm was sure to render it useless soon, anyway. Thunder crashed and the sky pelted torrents of rain as if God himself was weeping.

He trudged along the creek that wove like a swollen serpent across the pasture. Darkness made it difficult to see. He called Callie's name, heard others echoing his calls in the distance.

Somewhere in the darkness, Callie waited.

❧❧

Caroline's head was foggy, her heart like a wound bleeding out. She listened to the rain splatter the church roof, watched it slide like tears down stained glass windows that graced the length of walls along both sides of the sanctuary.

"Caroline." Sue touched her shoulder gently. "Matt said to take you home and let you get some rest. It's late and you're worn out."

"I'm not leaving. I *can't* leave."

Sue sighed. "Please, Caroline."

"No. Callie might come back here. I have to wait."

Sue followed Caroline's gaze to an oversized wooden cross hanging on the wall at the front of the sanctuary. She reached for her hand. "Would you like to pray?"

"I have been. But I don't know what else to say."

Sue squeezed her hand. "Then let me, OK?"

Tears spilled down Caroline's cheek as Sue prayed for the men searching, for Callie…and for her.

"Callie has her jacket," Caroline sobbed when Sue finished. "At least she has that."

"It's going to be OK." Sue stood and turned toward the kitchen. "I'll brew coffee and bring you something to eat."

Caroline merely nodded, too weary to argue.

Lulled by the patter of rain against the windows, Caroline's thoughts began to drift. Dreams enveloped her and warmed the chill in her bones.

A gentle touch on her shoulder drew her back to consciousness. Matt sat beside her. She placed a hand on his chest, felt the muscles beneath a damp T-shirt and knew he was real.

"Anything?" He was covered in mud from head to foot, and his pained, weary eyes told her all she needed to know. Caroline crumpled against him.

Matt slid his arms around her, sheltered her as sobs shook her. "I wish I could take the pain away," he murmured into her hair.

I want to be your fortress...

"Find her, please."

"Shh, honey," he soothed. "The rain has stopped, and it's going to be light soon. We'll have better luck then."

"Oh, Matt, what if..."

"God is taking care of Callie wherever she is. I know that with all my heart. He stroked her hair, soothed away tiredness and fear. "Andie and Paul have the horses, and I have to go meet them."

"I want to go with you, Matt."

"Caroline, you're exhausted."

"You are, too. I can't just sit here any longer. I need to *do* something."

"You *are* doing something. You're talking to God. That's the most powerful thing anyone can do."

"Pray with me, then." Caroline reached for his hand. "Please pray with me before you leave again."

Matt nodded. He sheltered her trembling hands in his and with renewed strength, they bowed their heads.

"Dear Heavenly Father," Matt's voice was gruff with emotion. "Please be with us all as we search for Callie. Shelter her in a safe place while she waits for us to come to her. Calm her fears, Lord, and let her feel Your presence. Guide our feet along a path straight to her, and return her safely to us soon. Thank you, Lord, for your never-ending mercy. Amen."

Matt's cell phone rang, startling them both. Caroline's belly roiled as he listened, then nodded stiffly and said, "I'm on my way."

∾∽

Matt rushed across the Aronson's property. A light shined in the barn. "What's going on?"

Paul paced the length of the stalls. "I'm not sure. Andie and I put Stormy in her stall an hour ago, just long enough to feed her while we changed into dry clothes. When we came back the stall door was open, and she was gone."

"I don't know how in the world she could have gotten the gate open," Andie added. "It's never happened before."

"I'm sure I latched it." Paul ran a hand through matted hair. "I even double-checked it, because I know Andie would have my hide if anything ever happened to that horse."

"Well, you two have been going for hours in the cold and rain, and you're both exhausted." Matt fingered the door latch, searching for clues. "Maybe you just thought you closed the stall."

"No, Matt. I checked it, too," Andie assured him. "And Kyle was with us. He would have noticed if the gate wasn't latched right."

"OK." Matt surveyed the muddy ground, pockmarked by hoof prints. "Do you think you can follow Stormy's trail, Andie? There are a lot of prints here. Some belong to Brown Bear, and maybe some of the other horses, as well."

"I know which are Stormy's," Andie convinced him. "I know as sure as I'm breathing."

"Let's go, then. Lead the way."

They fanned out, scanning the ground. As dawn broke, the sky began to clear. Sunlight bathed the road and pasture beyond in a milky glow. Andie quickly discerned Stormy's tracks from those of the other horses. The prints ambled across the paddock and down to the road. Matt could almost picture Stormy galloping through, her midnight-black mane swishing with the excitement of her escape.

Stormy had followed the road quite a way before her prints veered off sharply to the right and disappeared into a bank along the road. The clean scent of pine filled the air. Grass and pine needles blanketed the ground, and it was difficult to decide which way to go. The swollen creek rushed by with fury, and Matt prayed Callie had not been swept up and carried away in its wrath.

"What do you think?" He scanned his flashlight under bushes and along the rocky shore of the creek.

"Let's see..." Andie fell to her knees and patted a length of grass. "We should go this way."

"How do you know?"

"I can feel where Stormy's hooves left indentations. She's gone this way." She pointed to the right, up the bank and through a grove of pine trees. For the first time since the rain pummeled and pelted, Matt was glad for the downpour, because it rendered the ground pliable. But he was also thankful it had finally stopped, since any more saturation might have washed these precious clues away.

"Let's go, then." Matt was already heading in the direction Andie indicated. His stride ate up the ground. Every so often, he dropped to his knees to stroke the ground when the prints seemed to disappear.

"Keep searching," Matt encouraged, though frustration welled in him. Callie was still out there, cold, wet, and most likely terrified. The urgency to find her multiplied with each passing moment. "Spread out and search higher now. Look for broken tree limbs, anything Stormy might have displaced as she came by."

Paul branched off to the left, Andie to the right, and Matt plowed on straight ahead. The sound of their incessant cries for Callie blended with the chatter of birds waking to the cool dawn.

Matt slogged through damp, muddy earth covered in leaves and amber needles. The clean scent of pine gave him strength to take one more step forward. He'd promised Caroline. He couldn't let her down. *Oh, Lord, help me. Guide me to Callie.*

As the waking sun kissed dewy grass with warmth, Matt stilled and tried to sort through muddled thoughts. His body was numb with fatigue, his energy waning. His hands were bruised and bloodied from pushing through tree limbs and stroking the boggy ground. His breathing was labored and came in quick bursts that clouded the air. Exhausted, he pressed through yet another hundred yards of trees, his gaze searching the shadows. In the distance, he heard Paul's raw, strained voice calling for Callie.

Matt fought to quiet his breathing and still the quickening thump of his heart. A faint sound whispered on the rustle of leaves.

He paused, held his breath. The sound eased over the breeze once more. Adrenaline pumped as Matt found his footing and raced forward. His heart pounded with the exertion, and his breath fogged the morning air. He crested a hill and the grove of trees opened to glorious waves of cranberry sunrise flooding a taupe hay-filled pasture.

Nestled in the hay, Callie snuggled against

Stormy's side, sheltered from the wet and wind. The horse nickered softly. Her black eyes trained on Matt, then she dipped her head and nuzzled Callie like a protective mother.

Matt watched, stunned. He felt as though he was flying as he raced over the pasture toward them.

If he lived to be a hundred, Matt would never forget the incredible feeling when he fell to his knees beside Callie, and she turned her face up to gaze at him, eyes wide with innocent wonder.

"Matt?" She blinked hard twice, as if she might be dreaming.

"It's me, sweetie." He slid his palms gently along her limbs, checking for bumps and bruises. "Are you OK?"

She touched his face and smiled. "Oh, I found you."

Relief flooded Matt, and he hugged her. Hot tears blurred his vision. "Yes, you did." He peeled off his jacket and wrapped it snuggly around her, then gathered her into his arms. Stormy looked on with discerning eyes as if she fully understood the levity of the situation. Matt stroked her mane and pressed his cheek gently to Callie's damp blonde ringlets. The salt of his tears burned his eyes.

"It's OK now, Uncle Matt." Paul and Andie had come running. Paul clapped him on the back. "You found her."

"*We* found her," Matt corrected. He held Callie tighter, massaged the cold from her limbs.

"Oh, you spirited little imp!" Andie wrapped her arms around Stormy's neck and pressed her face into a matted coat. "How did you know where to find Callie?"

"She loves me," Callie explained, patting Stormy sleepily. "'cause I hug her and give her carrots and talk to her when she's lonely."

Matt kissed Callie's forehead. "I love you, too, sweetie. Let's take you to your mom. She's been waiting all night to see you."

"Ride Stormy," Paul suggested. "You'll get to the church faster on her than if you retrace your steps back to the truck and then drive there."

"Good idea." Matt handed Callie over to Paul long enough to mount the horse. Then he took Callie into his lap before grabbing the reins "Hold on, sweetie."

They made good time over the field, through a grove of trees, and along a section of the swollen creek until the church finally came into view. Its whitewashed steeple soared proudly into the clear morning sky.

Caroline met them at the edge of the property. Sunlight turned her hair into a halo of shimmering caramel, and the moment she saw them she rushed over the grass.

"Callie!" When Matt slid Callie into her arms, Caroline sank to the ground, rocking the child and sobbing with relief. "Oh, Callie."

"Happy Easter, Mama." Callie sighed and patted her face as if this was a typical Sunday morning event.

"Oh, my baby...Happy Easter."

Caroline reached for Matt's cold, muddy pant leg, gripping, tugging, until he slid from Stormy's back to join them in the damp morning grass.

"Thank you, Matt." The words came hard, forced through tears that streamed down her face. "Thank you for not giving up."

"Never." He wrapped his arms around Caroline as

she rocked Callie, and thanked God for this wonderful, miraculous gift.

ॐॐ

Slowly, Caroline and Matt deciphered the details of Callie's disappearance. Warmed with a breakfast of leftover burgers and cookies from the church kitchen, Callie chattered.

"I heard Paul and Andie talking about a treasure, and I wanted to see it." Callie sipped hot chocolate and smacked her lips.

"A treasure?" Caroline was confused. "Callie, I don't know what you're talking about."

"Wait a minute..." Andie tapped Paul's arm. "I think she means the treasure in the Bible verse we were discussing."

"Oh, yeah." Paul reached for a Bible in the seat beside him. "She means, 'Where your treasure is, there your heart will also be'. Chapter six, verse twenty-one in the book of Matthew. Andie and I were debating its meaning. Callie must have thought we were talking about a real treasure, like a chest of gold or something."

"Like with pirates," Callie chimed in. "I saw pictures in a library book. Isn't that what you were talkin' about, Paul?"

"No." He grinned and shook his head. "I'll explain it to you later. Just tell us what happened next."

"Well, I know I wasn't s'posed to, but I followed you." She hung her head. "I'm sorry, Mama. I guess I'm gonna get a time-out now, right?"

Caroline hugged her, still weak from the thought of losing her. "I haven't decided yet. We'll discuss your punishment later. Just go on."

Callie gulped. "Well, I tried to keep up. I'm pretty fast, you know. Mrs. Brabson said so. But Paul and Andie were going too fast. Then they stopped to kiss. *Yuck.*"

"What?" Matt and Sue exclaimed in unison.

Callie continued innocently. "Andie got a splinter in her hand from a branch, and Paul helped her get it out. Then he kissed her hand like this." She paused and reached for Matt's blistered hand. Turning it palm up, she kissed it tenderly. "He kissed away the boo-boo, like Mama does when I get hurt."

"Hmm..." Matt's brow furled as he glanced from Paul to Andie. "Not exactly G-rated, you two, but we'll get to that later."

"Yeah, OK." Paul looked like he wished the ground would open up and swallow him. "Go on, Callie."

"I sat down to wait for you 'cause my legs were real tired from runnin'. Then rain started to fall on my head, and it got so dark. I don't like storms." Her eyes filled with tears, and she trembled, remembering. "I was scared."

"Oh, Callie." Caroline took her into her lap and soothed with gentle hands. "It's OK now. You're safe."

"I crawled under a bush, but I still got all cold and wet. I kept yelling, but no one came."

"The storm was loud." Matt stroked the hair from her cool brow and kissed her forehead. "I'm so sorry, sweetie. We should have heard you."

"Then Stormy came. I thought I was dreaming. I snuggled up with her like I do with you when we watch a movie, Mama, and she got me warm. She talked to me with her special sounds, and I wasn't scared anymore." Callie paused, sipped hot chocolate, and continued. "Well, maybe just a little bit scared, but not *so* bad. I fell asleep, and when I woke up the sun was out, and Matt was calling me. He found me, Mama. I knew he would. The angels told me he would."

"The angels?"

"Oh, yes, Mama. They were all around me. That's how Stormy knew how to find me. She heard the angels."

18

The Easter service was delayed long enough for Pastor Jake to change into dry clothes. While they waited, members of the congregation drank coffee and visited. The women *oohed* and *aahed* over Callie while the men congratulated Andie and Paul for their part in finding her. And all of the children wanted a glimpse of the brave horse that grazed lazily behind the church, as if bored with it all.

She should be exhausted to the bone, yet Caroline felt energized. Sunlight spilled through stained glass windows over the choir loft where she waited for the service to begin. Sue and Matt had tried to convince her to go home and get some rest, but she could think of nowhere she'd rather be. Callie sat in Matt's lap, her eyes wide with wonder and exhaustion. She was flanked by Paul and Andie and the rest of the Aronson clan. Caroline knew there was no safer place for her daughter than to be sheltered in Matt's strong arms.

Matt had slipped into something dry, only because he had a change of clothes in his truck. But Paul and Andie were caked with a layer of dirt, and Caroline was sure they considered it a symbol of honor.

The organ sang and Pastor Jake rose to begin the service. He beamed and said, "You are the most beautiful congregation I've ever laid eyes on. I had an Easter sermon prepared for today, but it's been filed for another time. Because the events of the last twenty-four hours teach a lesson much greater than I could ever manage to relate."

Caroline smiled gratefully at Matt before her gaze slid to Callie, who snuggled contentedly in his loving embrace.

She heard Matt murmur to Callie. "Your mom's gonna sing for us now."

"She's gonna sing for God," Callie replied. "She sings like an angel."

"Yes, I know."

Caroline's voice felt raw and raspy, but her heart was bursting with thankfulness, so the words flowed smooth and powerful as rising waves. She truly understood who her Redeemer was. He'd given her a treasure here with Matt, surrounded by His love.

అం

Caroline settled into the porch glider and watched the sun set in a spectacular palette of orange and crimson. Gravel spat across the driveway, and she knew Matt had returned to her. A slow smile slid across her face as she rocked gently. A dusky breeze carried the scent of lilac.

"Hi, Caroline." Matt's broad shoulders were haloed by the setting sun. He paused at the foot of the porch stairs and drank her in. She felt renewed by a warm meal, a nap, and the knowledge that Callie slept soundly upstairs, tucked safely into her bed for the night.

Caroline studied his long, lean lines, caring blue eyes, and strong hands that calmed her with a gentle touch. "You look rested and...clean."

"Seems a hot shower works wonders following an all-night trek through muddy woods and soggy pastures." He laughed softly. "May I have the honor of sitting beside you?"

She scooted over. "I thought you'd never ask."

Together they rocked as crickets serenaded through waning sunlight.

"How's Callie?"

"Tired, hungry, cold, scared...but OK. She's convinced she's had the greatest adventure known to man with the highlight being her ride with you on Stormy."

"You should have seen her face, Caroline, when she saw me. It was the most amazing thing, the most incredible feeling."

"For her, too, I'm certain."

"How long's she grounded from the library?"

"What? Oh! I didn't have the heart. Not after all she's been through."

"Whew. Good."

Caroline laughed. "I think you're more relieved than she was."

"Maybe I am." He reached for her hand. "You're tough, Caroline. Tough but soft, too." He sighed and brushed her hair back. "You amaze me."

"Matt, I'm sorry for the way I've behaved toward you, for—"

"Hush." He pressed a finger to her lips. "No apology necessary."

"I should have been there for you and Paul after your accident, but I wasn't."

"You spent three days with me at the hospital. I needed you, and you were there."

"I mean after...when you came home. I was selfish

and scared, and I hurt you. Yet, when I needed you, you were there for me, no questions asked."

"I love you, Caroline."

"I don't blame you if—" The words registered. Her breath caught. "What did you say?"

"I said I love you, Caroline. I think I knew from the first time I saw you, when you plowed through the front door with a broom-handle in your hand."

"Oh." She gasped. "Oh!" She threw her arms around him. "And I love *you*, Matt. Oh, I do love you."

Epilogue

The weather could not have been more perfect for such a joyous gathering. A warm breeze kissed Caroline's cheeks as her long, silk gown shimmered beneath brilliant sunlight.

"Look, Mama, there's Matt." Callie beamed at the sight of him poised beneath the massive weeping willow that graced his property. Paul stood beside him, patting the pocket of his suit jacket for evidence of the rings tucked there.

Every so often Paul's eyes wandered to his mother, who'd flown in from Nashville to join them. Caroline knew he was adjusting to the idea of spending a little time with her. She'd always be a recovering alcoholic, but maybe they'd both learn that in her recovery they could rebuild a relationship of forgiveness and trust.

"Matt looks nice in that suit, Mama," Callie murmured. "What do you call it again?"

"A tuxedo, honey. And yes, Matt's very handsome." He made her heart ache with his kindness, his strength. "Let's go see him."

"It's time for you to get married, right?"

"That's right." She drew a deep, cleansing breath and thanked God once more for the many miracles he'd provided the past months. And the love she shared with Matt was the greatest miracle of all.

Callie dropped delicate pink rose petals into the summer grass to lead the way. When she approached Matt, he lifted her into the air and swung her around until she squealed with delight. Then he kissed her and planted her gently beside Caroline.

"Hi, there." He touched Caroline's hair through the veil of lace that framed her face. The spicy scent of his aftershave sent shivers down her spine.

"Hello."

"You look beautiful." She sensed he longed to kiss her, but knew he'd restrain himself—barely—as their friends waited for vows to be exchanged.

"Ready?" she asked, her heart overflowing.

"You bet."

They joined hands and turned to face Pastor Jake.

"Dearly beloved..." Caroline's mind wandered back to the day she and Callie had been so miserably alone in a terrifying storm...and they'd found Matt.

Or maybe Matt had found them.

All that really mattered was...they'd found each other.

CPSIA information can be obtained at www.ICGtesting.com

234255LV00001B/2/P